# SAUPTIK

## BLOOD AND FLOWERS

*via* AMRUTA PATIL

HarperCollins *Publishers* India

ह्रीं

It is the way of people to hack noses and breasts off old idols, to destroy lovingly raised heroes before they age into corrupt gods. The wisest sew old wisdom into their hem, though. They do it for the same reason that I pay close attention to forest lore about what feeds and what kills: empirical data gathered over the millennia is hard to piece together in a day.

This used to be a magnificent upside-down tree: its roots as expansive above as its canopy below. It drew sustenance from the stars and its fruit burst forth in soil. A deep rot has set in that makes the wood unreliable now. Perhaps it is best consigned to flames, but not before gazing once at what preceded the fester.

A caution, a key:
Don't impose your preconceptions onto the story and then claim objectivity.

EXPLOSIVE ORDNANCE DISPOSAL

Krshn ordered us to revoke the Pashupat astras we had drawn.
Arjun! Ashwatthama! Put an end to this nonsense immediately!

Arjun knew how to revoke the astra. I bore the curse of incomplete knowledge.
I can't do this -
I just don't remember how.

Krshn intervened. The astras were pulled back. Explosive ordnance disposal.

I should take your foolish head back for Draupadi. But how will you learn anything without it?

He reached out, plucked the jewel out of my forehead.

He knew I had been burning. That ember had been lodged deep in me since the day I was born. I imagined it must sparkle with the clear notes of a ruby.
Wander all alone for three thousand years. Make sure you use your time well.
Surviving the war was collateral damage. I should have died on Kurukshetra with everyone else I knew. Instead, marked by a gouge-wound, I was sent into insignificance and solitude, into strange epochs peopled by strangers.

One's own death is easy. Being witness to a surfeit of violent deaths is harder because it blunts the receptors that keep us human. When you meet him as yet another rotting carcass, it's hard not to avert your eyes from your own brother.

There are seven other chiranjeevis in the remembered history of the worlds. Asur Bali, who offered his head to Vishnu to place his foot on. The perfectly subdued monkey mind, Hanuman. My maternal uncle, Kripa. The avatar Parshuram. Ravan's brother, Vibhishan. Vyas rishi. And me. Of the seven, I'm the only one on whom preternatural long life was slapped on as a curse, not a blessing – for that's what immortality is without the gift of forgetting. I wait for my term to end.

OUTLIERS

I smell of stale blood and unwashed rags. Ganga was cool, silvery. People were struck by her. She storied their lives but spoke in abstractions few understood the urgency of. When she left, she named me sutradhaar.
If you have sense, listen.
They waited around for some hours.
Uh. Are you ever going to speak?
What a horrid smell.
I can't speak. Can't coax one word out of my throat, nor recall how a voice ought to leave the cavern of the chest and sound itself in air.

Someone pelts me with a stone. It sets the forehead bleeding again.
Bottom feeders! Would you know a hero if he came to you in an unexpected body?
Facial wounds weep copiously and look far more grave than they really are. Another stone gets me in the face. This isn't going well. I have to leave.

I duck into the underbrush where no beast can give me chase. My eyes are perfectly calibrated to low light. I can see better in darkness than in light. Light brings clutter. I know the shadows like no other being does.
Toop* toop!
The crow pheasant gives me company. They call him Bharadwaj in these parts. After my family. Why? Because he scrambles in the underbrush like I do, plaintively begging, 'toop toop', like I beg for ghee to soothe my wounds.

*Ghee

On the smashan grounds, there is warmth and unobtrusive companionship. There is also ghee for my wound. Extinguished bodies brought here night and day make one thing clear: you need to honour the living as much as you lament the dead. That I haven't spoken to them for years but found my tongue today, the pyre-keepers find amusing, not startling. (They aren't startled by much.) They toss me a shroud to cover my cock – for the benefit of the townsfolk. Yes, Langda and Bhainga have always been generous. They know a corpse has no more use for a shroud than it does for ghee.

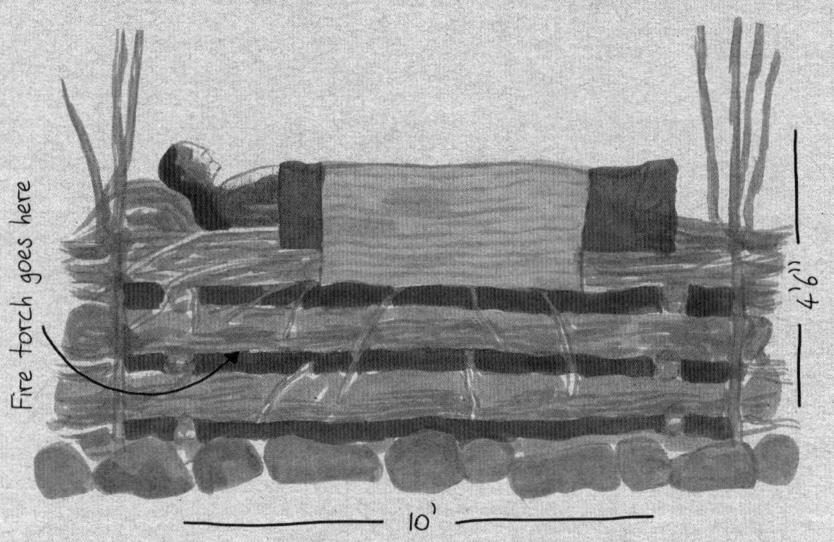


I wasn't always without a tongue. For many years, I was the madman ranting ferociously in town squares, while people stopped to listen. Kings and minions alike feel safe listening to crazy people. Crazy wisdom is injected straight into the vein. You know it's true even when it insults you, but there is no loss of face because, after all, who is it that rages? Just a madman.

There came a time when kings stopped listening. I slipped into quietitude so I wouldn't be dragged away and beaten up. During drought, there's no time for abstraction. And it's hard to tell sage from madman.

Over the millennia, Agni has glutted on so many buckets of ghee, he is sickened by it. He craves other offerings – dry wood, lean bodies, hubris – anything but ghee. The relationship between a man and his yagna fire-pit is a deeply personal one. Neither priest nor spouse has any role to play. The yagna site is chosen and readied with love, but it is temporary. When the sacrifice is over, Agni sated, embers extinguished, the site is swept clean. Ashes are cast in the river. All traces of man-fire intercourse are wiped away.
Next time around, you start afresh.

This is why the purpose of permanent idol houses (the sort popular now) escapes my understanding. The only temple we were allowed was the one above our brows; the only sacrifice, that of our own body and being.

On the other side of the social wall, a huge show is made of celebrating Shiv. Bigots and conformists alike imitate his posture and paraphernalia, but this is as far as they can go because understanding his essence is much more work. Lazy devotees of this Lord of Beasts are quick to make outcasts out of oddballs. Let alone adoration, even basic courtesy is hard to muster when you meet a real outlier. Would you recognize a god who wore the wrong body?

Real outliers are inconvenient because they can lie well beyond the periphery of your imagination. Shiv spent most of his days in the high-altitude desert that was Mount Kailash. When he did come down to the plains, he set up camp on smashan grounds where ghouls and scavengers wandered.

He was Pashupati, Lord of Beasts. Like the beasts did he wander, naked but for a layer of ash smeared on his body. Did the ashes come from burnt wood or carcasses? Between fingers, it is difficult to tell the difference.
In offering boon or curse, Shiv made no distinction between dev-asur, sinner or sage. He sought neither comfort nor validation. No apsara could distract him long enough for him to spill his semen. He made no difference between fresh and rotten, berry and entrails. When he ate, he took no second helpings.

Of all prajapatis in the multiverse, Daksha was the most prominent. He had countless wives and daughters. His daughters all chose their own mates and became the mothers of devas, asurs, birds, animals, plants, constellations – cousins, all. Daksha doted on all his daughters, but Sati was his favourite.
I choose Shiv.

The most effective ways to send data into the future? To reproduce. To teach. To leave seeds buried to awaken in time, at the right moment.

Daksha believed in virile engagement. Narad muni, flitting between worlds and causing havoc in the minds of the oversure, didn't believe in it. Daksha hated Narad for having swayed his sons into renunciation. The two never saw eye-to-eye.

The being Sati chose as her mate was even more preposterous than Narad. The shock Daksha experienced when Sati announced Shiv's name! Shiv's severe abode, macabre entourage, his insouciance towards social conventions made him infamous among the genteel. The ultimate outlier, Shiv was Daksha's ultimate nightmare. Sati remained resolute in her choice of mate. Daksha retaliated by cutting off all contact with her.

Among Kailash's craggy peaks, Sati did what no one had managed to before her. She made the recluse sit up and take notice of what was outside him.
I'm hungry and bored.
Play with me, Bholenath.
Reminded of the world, Shiv made his way down to Kashi and domesticity. Sometimes he tired of playing house, retreated to his old ways. But the hermit had become a householder. He always came back to his beloved.

Some years later, Sati found out her father was holding a yagna to honour the most important rishis in the multiverse. Shiv was not on the guest list.



Daksha's approval or disapproval meant absolutely nothing to Shiv. But it did hurt Sati, who still harboured naïve hopes of winning her father over.

Daksha knew his strange son-in-law's calibre better than anyone else, but he didn't want to acknowledge him publicly. Shiv's nonchalance unsettled him. He treated the mighty prajapati like he treated anyone else: unless addressed directly, Shiv did not notice Daksha at all. Of all the rishis at the yagna, only Dadhichi talked about Shiv's absence. Daksha paid him no heed.
Your husband is so uncouth, he wouldn't even find lodging in the goat sheds here.

It would be accurate to say Sati combusted from shame and disappointment. When word travelled to Kailash, Shiv's bhoot gana descended and completely destroyed Daksha's sacrifice, snuffed out the yagna fire. They were a frightening lot, the likes of whom a restrained, genteel society couldn't even conceive of, much less overpower. A white-hot Shiv beheaded his father-in-law. Daksha would be eventually revived, but with the head of a goat, not of a man. He'd live the rest of his days with a souvenir of his own arrogance, and of an outlier's wrath.

Those killed by Shiv are often revived with animal heads. Marked by the Lord of Beasts, they are finally free to lead uncomplicated lives. The more you are led by your head, the likelier that you will need to be (metaphorically) beheaded. Says Pashupati, don't forget your place in the schema, biped mammal.
Lose your head! Be sweet and unself-conscious!

Shiv remained inconsolable for aeons, walking around with Sati's corpse held aloft his shoulder. He neglected everything and everyone else.

So great was Shiv's apathy, Bhoo Devi froze. No sapling could crack her surface. Until Shiv clung to the mortal remains of his beloved, there could be no closure or relief. Vishnu had to intervene, make Sati's corpse disintegrate.

Wherever a piece of Sati's body fell, a seat of feminine power emerged.
Eventually Shiv met Parvati, who had all of Sati's grace but none of her fragility. Parvati had a wrathful aspect she did not hesitate to show.

There's an uncomplicated honesty about my disreputable companions. Langda had a wooden stump for a left leg which got tossed onto a dying pyre during his last drunken bout. We sit around warmed by the cadaver of a flower-seller.

Your Shiv is so scrawny.

He was a hermit, not a mithai-vendor.

He's as scrawny as you need him to be. As ashen. Or blue. Or muscular.

Silence is a hard habit to give up. Each enunciated word is an effort. I tell one story, but as many versions will be heard as there are people before me. I can never be sure what they will hear.

One day, Prajapati of the golden womb was surrounded by devas, asurs and mortals of the seeking sort. They awaited revelation, simply wouldn't leave.

O Father-Mother! Show us the way!

For what felt like forever, Prajapati didn't stir. Then he made a sound. Was it a dyspeptic grunt? Syllable of cosmic import? Was he just fooling around?

Da.

The asurs reflected upon that.

Da?

He's telling us to work on our Dama, restraint.

No lesson more vital than to subdue vain ambition.

The devas, too, thought about the significance of Prajapati's grunt all the way home. No lesson more urgent than to ease their tightly clenched fists.

Da must mean Daan, charity.

Mortals contemplated Prajapati's Da too.

He wants us to work on Dayaa, compassion.

They found that harder than anything else under the sun.

# MAN WITHOUT A COW

Natal stories often feature distracted rishis and distracting apsaras; seed spilled into unconventional matrices. Both my parents had odd births, as did most significant people in this tale. Why so? To emphasize the importance of mutations and systemic oddness, perhaps.

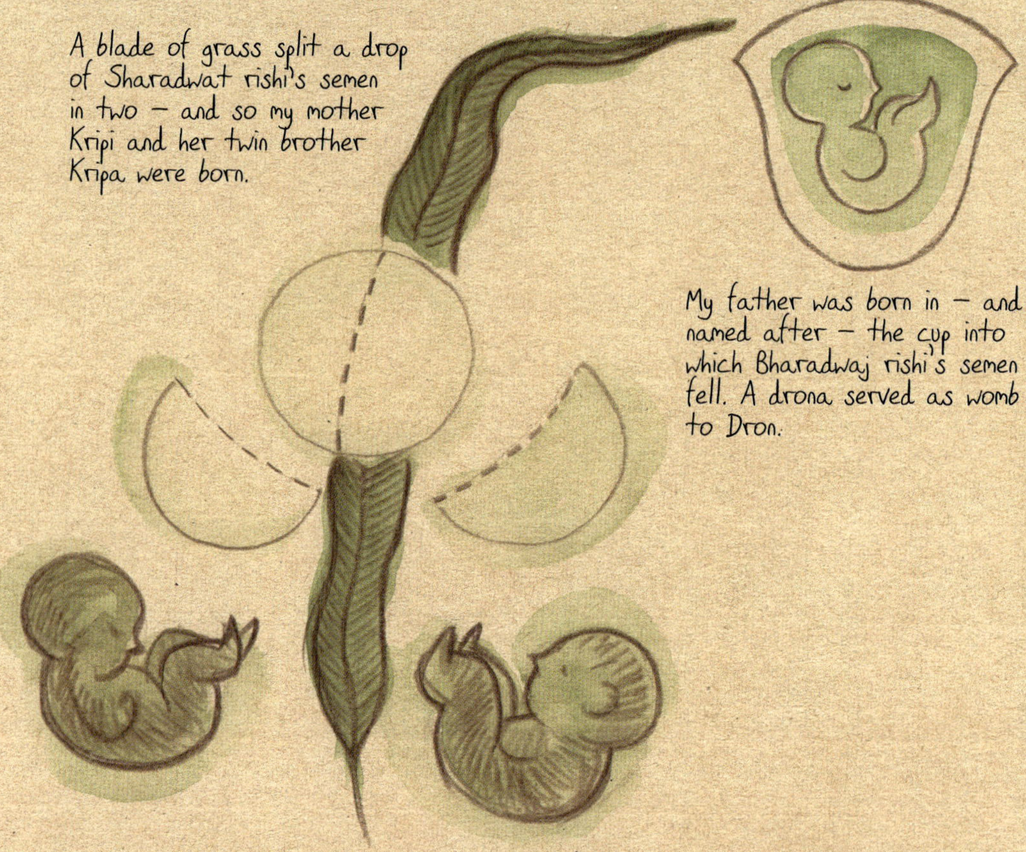


My natal story was unremarkable aside from the fiery ember in my forehead. Our lineage is a fiery one. Generations have made oblations to Agni, invoking him in the name of land and child, granary and coffer, rivalry and conquest. With such a fire fixation, scorch and heartburn were only to be expected.

My father, sole lineage bearer of Angiras's tradition, who received divine astras from Parshuram himself, was a brahmin without a cow in his yard. We ought to have had a cow in our yard, far less worthy people did. Free-grazing cows mean autonomy: milk, fuel, ghee for the asking. Land feeds cow, cow feeds land, and the one who tends to them gently is fed by both.

Drupad, prince of Panchal, studied in Agnivesh's gurukul like my father. Both adept at invoking the agni astra, they were the best of friends.
Okay.
What I own is half yours.
It was only an impulsive promise on Drupad's part, but Dron – who never said what he didn't mean – held others to the same standard, somewhat foolishly. Drupad's words remained etched in his mind, trump card for a rainy day.

Cut to decades later, the day our family's fate changed over a cup of milk. I didn't know what cow's milk tasted like until we went to Hastinapur. The boys once fed me rice flour mixed in water, said it was milk. I believed them.
Ashwatthama, are you sure you know what a cow looks like, even?
It was thread-worn heckling, but I cried anyway. This upset my mother.
Of what use is your learning and greatness, if it cannot afford your family one cow?
It always begins like that.

He told her the story of the soft-hearted hermit who took a stray kitten in. It mewled all night from hunger and made the hermit quite restless.
He used all his money to buy a goat so the kitten could have some milk.
The goat proved to be an unruly one. The hermit found a wife to manage the bedlam. That everyone could be comfortable, he built a house. That he could sustain the lifestyle, he stopped being a hermit, got a job.

In the way children do, I took the blame square on my shoulders. Had I not cried for milk, mother wouldn't have scolded father, he wouldn't have gone to Drupad for help. No insult, no vow of vengeance, no Hastinapur, no Arjun.
Share your kingdom with me like you promised, friend. We'll be invincible together!
Ask for wealth. I'll give you more than you can carry. But friendship is between equals, Dron. You aren't my equal!
Power breeds maggots in the soul. I will be back, I promise. And I will bring you ruin.
Drupad was no Bali to offer his head as alms to a brahmin. He had the heft and preoccupations of a mighty king now. My father's artlessness irritated him.

This was the protocol back in the day:
Bow to the elder.
Bless the youngling.
Embrace the equal as friend.
Elder doesn't mean Older. It means someone who is more evolved. Staying alive longer gets easier by the day. Not all grey whiskers merit reverence.

Dron's threat troubled Drupad. He looked at his and Prishati's children, and saw no match for Dron. Shikhandi did have the mettle, to be fair. Born female, she chose to live as a male. But Dron had vowed not to hurt a woman. The old fogey would refuse to fight Shikhandi on a technicality.
I will shatter Dron to bits if you let me.
We must pray to Agni for a son –
You want a missile, not a son. I refuse to be a part of this.
In Prishati's stead, yagna flames served as womb for Agni's scorching seed. In effect then, Agni was father AND mother to Drupad's new progeny.

From the fire emerged Drishtadyumn fully grown, fully armed. He wasn't alone. Krshna Draupadi emerged, as fiery and hypnotic as the element she came from.
If you lived anywhere that wasn't under a rock, it was impossible not to have heard of Drupad's twins or their mission to destroy my father. In time, Drishtadyumn was sent to my father to learn the martial tradition –

Drupad sent his son to train with the foe because he trusted his honour and calibre as a teacher. Dron, on his part, trained his future assassin willingly and knowingly. Drishtadyumn was taught all that was required to bring Dron down. Can you even begin to imagine these mad-sounding scenarios? It falls into place when you look at the entire tapestry on the loom instead of focusing on the details.

I'd have told this story differently three thousand years ago. The events were raw and I, so angry. Temperance in others can be a bore, temperance in oneself a chore. Angry heroes are easy to understand, that's why they gather such a following.

Why was a brahmin so full of personal ambition? Why did a man of learning turn a slight into a lifelong mission of vengeance? Why would an undeluded man think a king owed him half an empire? Why? Because in most men, siddhi is not wisdom, it is poison.

# LET THE PHENOMENA PLAY

On the coils of an infinite serpent, Vishnu sleeps. Luscious sap of sattva stirs within him, a single lotus emerges from his navel, and a world begins.

Devas and asurs, warring cousins, churn the ocean for amrit. Shree emerges during the churning, bounties of the earth personified. Ignoring all smitten dev-asurs, the devi picks Vishnu and takes her place – not at his feet or side but inside his solar plexus. Earth goddess Bhoo lives with Vishnu too.
Bovine Bhoo
Lotus-born Shree
Vishnu's bond with the devis is for keeps. They won't abandon him, nor he, them.

Bhoo often manifests as a cow. Every kalpa, the brutality of world-seizers leaves her bruised, udders chapped, flanks lacerated and bleeding. She seeks Vishnu's help. Often, her pursuers are basically good folks who just don't know any better until they are taught. King Prithu was one such.
He learned how Bhoo liked to be milked: gently, by the best of hands. Such a good learner was he, mrityulok came to be known as Prithvi after Prithu.

During a periodic tug-of-war to restore balance in mrityulok, devas and asurs manifested as the princes of Hastinapur and their allies; Vishnu as the avatar Krshn; Earth, Wind, Fire and Water as the elemental Pandavs.
Shree and Bhoo manifested as Draupadi – wife of the Pandavs. Intrigues aplenty would unfold, but the moment Hastinapur's demise became inevitable was when Draupadi was humiliated. A world that does not treat Shree and Bhoo with respect and tenderness is a world on the brink.

There were other worlds before, there will be others hence. All end in flood and fire. The ocean's surface is flecked with the ashes of destroyed worlds.
Between the end of one world and the beginning of the other, Vishnu sleeps.

It was Ganga who ribboned through the narrative so far. With the avatar Krshn's birth, a different river takes over as companion to this tale. Her name is Yamuna, Yami, twin sister of Yama, lord of death. As dark and turbulent as the Dwapar Yug she flows in, Yamuna will shadow the story loyally.
Things were atypical this time round. Vishnu manifested in mrityulok not as a ruler but as a cowherd. His primary way of relating wouldn't be as warrior or king, but as love object. He'd be beloved baby, beloved friend. Beloved.

Born under Rohini nakshatra, he was named Krshn for his dark skin. Vasudev and Devaki, his parents, ensured he was raised in anonymity so he'd survive a threat to his life from his uncle Kamsa, King of Mathura. Vasudev set out towards Gokul on a rainy night, baby in hand. As he waded into the Yamuna, the capricious river went still, parted her waters for his safe passage.
Never forget the river's kindness –
Only once did Yamuna raise an impulsive splash, to kiss Krshn's toes.

Krshn was kept in the cradle of Nand and Yashoda, a cowherd couple in Gokul. Their baby daughter Yog Maya was taken to Mathura as a stand-in.
Some say Yog Maya, slippery as a fish, evaded Kamsa's murderous hands and flew away. Some say she was turned to compost for the health of the land.

Garud drishti, raptor's panoramic view. Sarpa drishti, serpent's eye for detail. The avatar's gaze didn't alternate between one and the other. It contained both.

Devaki wept when Krshn was born. His birth made her sad because she knew she couldn't keep him for herself even briefly. Neither could his foster mother Yashoda. Nor Radha, who loved him first. Nor the rest of the gopis who loved him as much as Radha did. Nor Rukmini, nor Satyabhama nor all of his other wives no one can remember the names of. Even Draupadi, his sakhi, couldn't claim Krshn for herself, nor could his sakha, Arjun.

Most people are more interested in possessing exclusive rights to the beloved than in knowing or benefiting from the beloved. Krshn belonged to no one. Krshn belonged to anyone who reached out to him. To be proprietary was to grasp at fistfuls of sand. Those who outgrew grasping spoke of a state of continuous benediction. From the mundane to the monumental, Krshn's attention to detail was constant.

They came of their own volition. He teased the gopis, enchanted them, let them do with him as they willed. Some days, they adorned him with flowers and peacock feathers, dressed him up in their jewels and in women's clothes.
They played with him, and he delighted in their delight.

The human body instinctively knows percussion and wind instruments. Shiv's damru is the thump-a-lump of the beating heart. Krshn's flute, the bansuri, has as many orifices as the human body. Breath that animated the bansuri brought Braj bhoomi alive. Theirs was an uncomplicated devotion, and the gopas and gopis found their loving gaze returned in full measure.

Come as you are. Or don't come at all.
All veils were dropped around Krshn. Politeness, shame, shyness, coquetry – he saw through them all. Those attached to veils find this state terrifying.

Krshn was no Shiv-in-ashes. His body was mortal but beautifully scented and anointed and clad. Vishnu's insignia were his to summon at will.

Sudarshan Chakra, the wheel of time, to cull delusion.

Conch to sound a loud announcement, warning.

Mace to end hubris.

Flowers to bring alert beauty to any setting.

The greatest beings to walk the world are often gardeners of beauty.

Framed in silver hyperbole, these stories linger. Krshn was loathe to take up arms as an adult, but his childhood was a mix of bucolic and wrathful. The list of noxious beings was long, and Krshn started subduing them early. His first kill was Vishkanya Putana, comely assassin sent by his uncle Kamsa.
Putana's beautiful breasts were plump with poison.
When she held him close, Krshn put his mouth to Putana's nipple. He sucked until milk, blood and the very essence of Putana drained away. What was left of her resembled the papery sheath that covers ashwagandha berries.

Then came the turn of the vicious hood, Kaliya.
Kaliya had poisoned Yamuna, turned her water oily and opaque. He let no man or beast approach her. Instead of killing the serpent, Krshn danced on his hood until all cockiness was squashed. Yamuna and Krshn's bond grew closer.

Krshn watched his people neglect their cows and pastures to prepare lavish offerings for Indra every year. The gopas and gopis were scared of Indra, his aloofness that parched the land, the deluges that washed away top soil and rotted the hooves of their cattle and the grain they ate.
Why do you beg for validation?
You are cowherds. Be sweet to your cows, to Mount Govardhan who gives shelter and pasture. Don't bother about anything else.

Livid at being denied attention, Indra brought on his infamous deluge.

Krshn lifted Mount Govardhan from its roots, perched it on his little finger.
To all gathered creatures, he gave shelter from the storm.

Man holds aloft mountain on his pinkie finger. It's the sort of display that says, 'Goodbye uncomplicated love, hello sycophants and needy acolytes'.
Krshn effaced the memory of his own magnitude from peoples' minds.
Even Vinata's son, blindingly golden Garud, had to shrink himself to a non-threatening form so people wouldn't be overwhelmed. These are concessions a teacher must make to ensure seekers focus on the lesson at hand.

They were all older now. The gopis were even more in love with Krshn, if that were possible. On a full moon night, when oceans and saplings alike stand on tiptoe to reach up high, things stirred in a most odd way in Braj bhoomi.
Notes from Krshn's bansuri rose.
The gopis' thoughts flew towards the forest in the middle of the night. It was a private smiting, so secret it wouldn't confide in the closest sakhi.

Unbeknownst to one another did the gopis make their way to a forest grove.
They could not – would not – be restrained.

Leaving behind sleeping husbands and darkened homesteads, gopis young and old walked into the night. They needed no torch light to lead them to the beloved.

Unbeknownst to one another did the gopis stand at the heart of the grove, hearts beating so hard, you could see the pounding at pulse and jugular.
Unbeknownst to one another did each gopi find her Krshn in the grove.

Each gopi separated from the next by one Krshn; each with her own Krshn throbbed in circular dance. Slowly, slowly. Faster, faster. Higher, higher –

– until they fused to a single point. Mount Meru of pure de-light!
Next morning, sleeping homesteads stirred in Braj bhoomi. Weary feet, lost anklets, enduring bliss, but no clear memory of the dancing night bygone.

Not everyone thought of Krshn as love object. His legend didn't conquer the land during his lifetime. But stories did travel and a small rash of curiosity grew. Some were drawn to his person, some were jealous. Others, like Vasudev Paundraka, copied Krshn's ways and tried to pass them off as their own.
Bring me my flute, you!
Egged on by sycophants and courtiers of limited intelligence, Paundraka soon imagined himself to be more Krshn than Krshn himself. He sought a fight.
The Sudarshan Chakra is mine and Krshn must return it immediately.

Send back my chakra right away and take refuge with me, Krshn.
If it's yours, you must have it. Here.
The chakra beheaded Paundraka and returned to rest lightly on Krshn's finger.

Now more than ever, when my mind retreats to grottos of beauty and familiarity, it is Krshn's childhood and youth I take refuge in, not my own. His days feel like my own clothes, although I did not wear them in this lifetime. The sense is of recognition, not borrowing. I KNOW these things.

For all the punctuations of sweetness in my own life – there were some – I know we were just grains of sand blowing into the vortex of Kurukshetra. We weren't flowers being nurtured, we were arrowheads being sharpened.

I see what's rolling, but I can't relate. Bhakti makes people soft in the head.
Langda likes switchblade more than gigglefest!
What would you make of your lived days? Battlefield or playing field? The question returns again and again, and from these two options must you pick.

# DADHICHI'S SPINE

My father came to the gates of Hastinapur bearing a fate-changing grudge, found work as a teacher to Dhritrashtra's brood. Not long after, Pritha and her five Pandav sons came to the gates of Hastinapur, bearing the mortal remains of Pandu. The bones were pristine, picked clean of the stain of living.
King Dhritrashtra had his brother's remains cremated with full ceremony but noticed the omen: they were dealing with the bones of a good man.

It was the bones of a good man that pierced the bloat of Vritra. To supply some backdrop: Tvastra, maker of divine armaments and baubles, had a son whom Indra beheaded. To avenge this, Tvastra created a magical serpent immune to all astras, to parch Indra of the water-fire that defined him.
Vritra swallowed all the water in existence, became juicy and autonomous. No moist clouds, no rain, no rivers. Oceans turned into dry, sunken beds.

Indra panicked. Brahma suggested he bring Vritra down with a non-divine weapon. Raw material for this clever non-divine weapon needed to be supplied by a most unusual man. It was Dadhichi rishi they chose for the culling. Mrityulok's only non-negotiable premise is 'Be fed, then be food'. Dadhichi's staggering tapasya had earned him something no other man had: mritsanjeevni, knowledge that could revive people from death. That such powers rested with a mortal upset the order of things.

Dadhichi HAD to be brought down.
Vritra's drought was only an alibi.

There was a catch, though. Dadhichi was immune to death at another person's hand. He needed to bring himself down! What seems like an impossible absurdity turned out to be easy enough. Having known both death and the other thing, Dadhichi had no desire to cling to life. When Indra asked for his bones, the rishi gave up his body with a laugh. Out of his spine was fashioned an electric pillar, a thunderbolt known as the Vajra. It would be Indra's signature weapon.

Vritra couldn't withstand the force of the Vajra. The thunderbolt split open the serpent, released the trapped waters, scattered into countless pieces.
Fragile order was restored, for the moment.

Bhoo Devi will eventually take back everything she gave you – every drop of water, every morsel of bone and sinew – but she likes it when beings don't need to be taken down kicking and screaming. Unsurprisingly, Bhoo looked upon Dadhichi's sacrifice fondly: it was bone meal supplied by a good man.
Each splinter of this son's spine will bring electric vitality to the soil where it falls.

Hastinapur knew another man like Dadhichi. Its founder, King Kuru, came upon land bracketed by the rivers Saraswati and Yamuna and knew his fate to be tied with it. Kuru lodged his golden plough in soil, proclaimed it to be his capital. His ambitions were odd for a rajanya-on-the-make. Kuru dreamed not just of empire and glory, but of a land with eight nodes abuzz.
I hope eight seeds take root here –
Self-control!
Sacrifice!
Truth!
Tapas!
Compassion!
Forgiveness!
Clarity!
Charity!

What will you feed the land so it raises such ambitious crop?
I will feed myself to the land if I must.
Predictably insecure, Indra had come by to heap jealous scorn on Kuru.

Vishnu stopped by to ask Kuru the same question.
And where do you hope to find such high-grade seeds?
In my own body, if I have to.
Extend the hand you'd sow these seeds with.
Vishnu lopped Kuru's right hand into pieces. Kuru extended his left hand, it was chopped into bits as well. As were his arms, his feet, his thighs and torso.

When it was the turn of his head, Kuru did not flinch. Vishnu was pleased.



Mrityulok cannot be granted any forevers, or else Kuru would not have been denied. He was promised this: as long as Hastinapur's kings remained worthy, Vishnu and Shiv would watch over the land. In tandem. When things eroded, time was up, they would raze Kuru's lineage clean to the ground. In tandem.

True to his word, Vishnu and Shiv remained in the warp and weft of Hastinapur. Vishnu's was the way of the careful garden, Shiv's was the way of the compost pit. To Vishnu, putrefying compost is a potential garden. Shiv sees a lush garden as potential compost. The Shiv stories I have told you were meant to set the stage for his counterpart Vishnu. Vishnu-Krshn led Hastinapur to engagement. Shiv-Mahadev led it to dissolution.

~

Exhausted by the capriciousness of mortals, river Saraswati retreated underground. Her imprint can still be seen from the skies, and in the unbroken lore. Yamuna remained above ground, reluctant to abandon Krshn, her waters growing darker and darker with Dwapar and Kali Yug's turbulence.

I find myself thinking of two belles encountered many moons ago; the only people there who could look beyond my unkempt form. Neti Neti and Iti Iti they were called. 'Not This, Not This'. 'This! And This!'
Austere sister and hedonistic sister, peering at one another across a wall. Each kept the other in check: from abstemious parch, from festering excess.

# PLUMB LINE

When Pandu died, his younger wife Madri gave up her life, leaving her twin sons in Pritha's care. Pritha guarded all five boys fiercely, making no distinction between those born of Madri's womb and those born of hers.
Bheem-Arjun can look out for themselves –
Take care of the twins. The world is too wily for them.
The paternity of the boys – born of four different fathers – was whispered about. Pritha refused to dignify rumours with response. The boys won everyone over with their humility and charm. Gossip and backstories were forgotten.

* Ambika and Ambalika

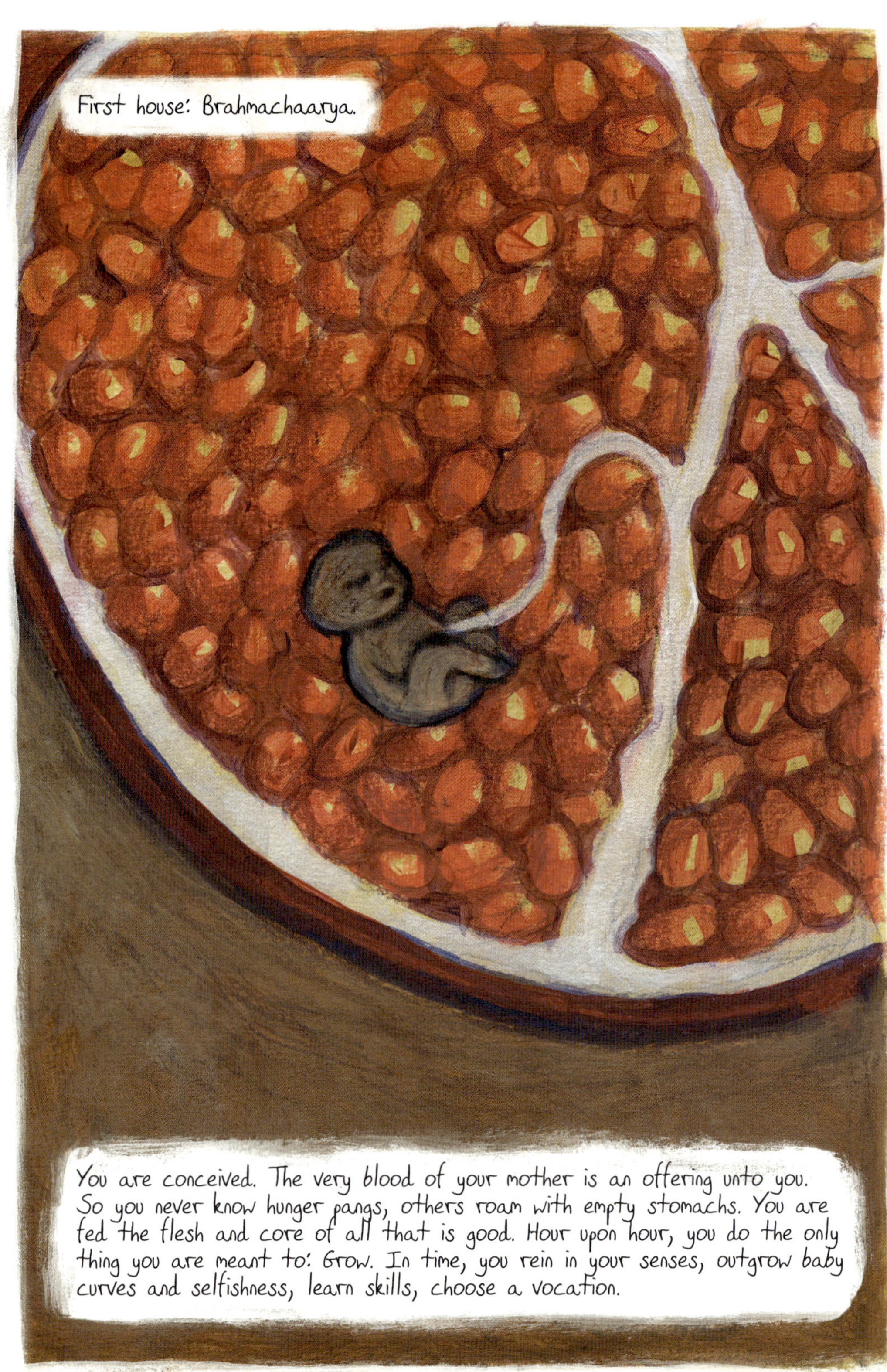
First house: Brahmachaarya.
You are conceived. The very blood of your mother is an offering unto you. So you never know hunger pangs, others roam with empty stomachs. You are fed the flesh and core of all that is good. Hour upon hour, you do the only thing you are meant to: Grow. In time, you rein in your senses, outgrow baby curves and selfishness, learn skills, choose a vocation.

Second house: Grihasta.
Long of stride, capable of reach, you are the nurturer now. You loosen the tight topknot of the first house, choose a loving mate, enjoy all the pleasures a too-short lifetime has to offer. What you gather must be shared with those at your table, those seeking alms at your door.

Third house: Sanyaas.
From lead actor, learn to be supporting cast. Abdicate your throne so the children may grow up. Let the succulent fruit and blood of your body be an offering unto others. Eat what the tree discards and what the wind brings to your feet. The gaze changes to vatsalya, your career as predator is over. Wean yourself, curl inward, there is no need to gather anymore.

Tended to by generations of doms,* the fire-pit has been kept alive without interruption since this city came into being. People queue up with corpses for a clutch of grass ignited at the dom's fire. His work is important enough that folks will pay good coin for it. But it does involve touching bodies riddled with malaise and cracking open skulls to set souls free – enough to ensure people keep a terrified distance once the bodies are offloaded.

The dom raja's most striking physical feature is unhappiness. His dead father wore an identical unhappiness. The burning ground brought wealth, but the wealth brought no access. In the city of the ultimate smashan-dweller Shiv, doms are gilded pariahs. The dom raja can smell burning flesh even in his dreams.

Fire, however, makes no distinction between couth and uncouth. Dead king and dead donkey are taken with equal detachment. Agni will reduce them both.

* Community that oversees cremations

We are being warmed by a dead perfume-vendor today.
What did you do before you ended up here?
I was left behind here after someone's cremation when I was a toddler.
Bhainga's folks didn't even wait for Yamraj to do his bit! I came here to prevent my stepfather from breaking my remaining leg.
The dom raja doesn't wait around once the first fire is applied to a pyre. Tending to the flames is the job of my oddball companions. In return, they get food and a place to sleep. At dawn, Langda scavenges through ashes for coins, rings, fillings. Bhainga makes a quiet coin selling unstained blankets the corpses come wrapped in. They share their earnings.

I was a warrior trained by the greatest teacher alive. To fathom the true nature of a warrior's tale, you must understand our training. No disrespect, but you can't gauge it by a tailor's rulebook or a grocer's honour code. Our metier, our mode of expression, was death. Dealing out death to others, and knowing how to meet one's own.

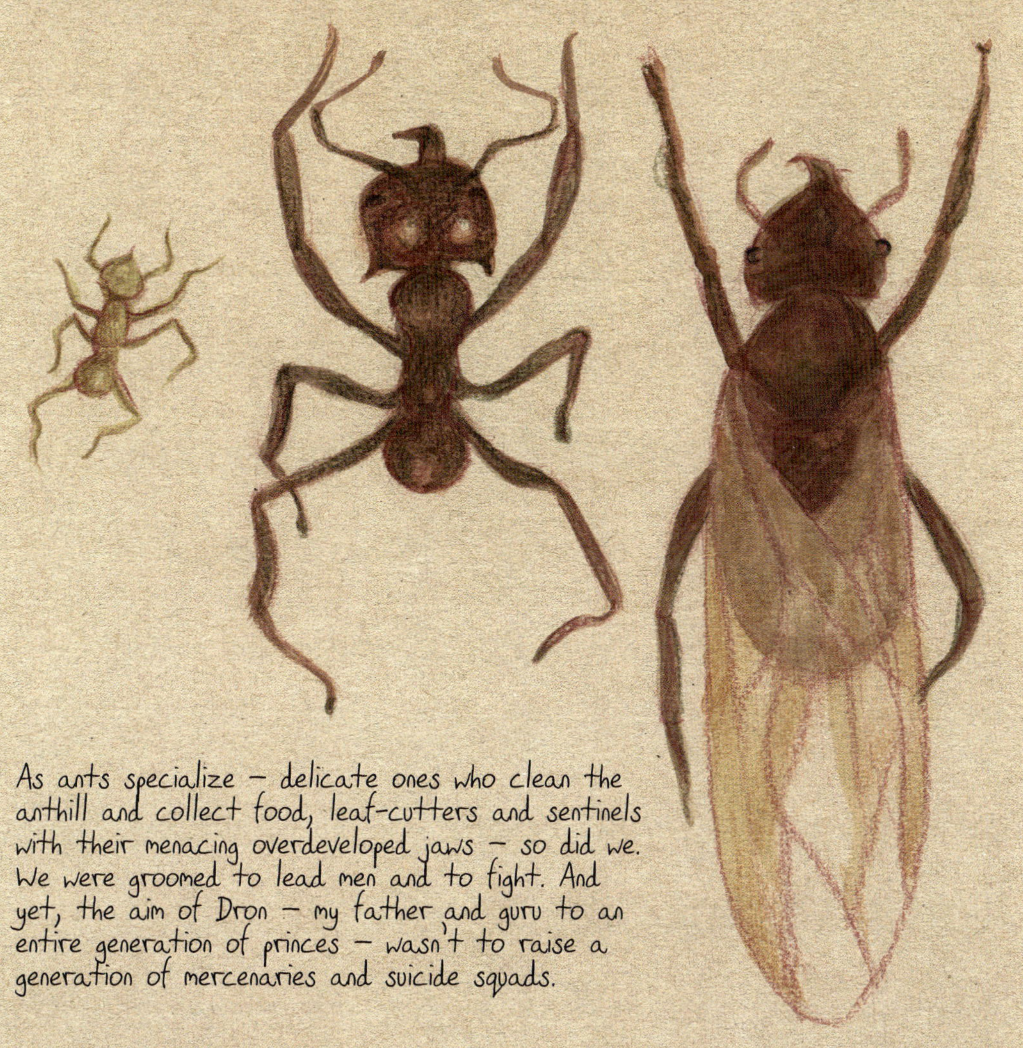

As ants specialize – delicate ones who clean the anthill and collect food, leaf-cutters and sentinels with their menacing overdeveloped jaws – so did we. We were groomed to lead men and to fight. And yet, the aim of Dron – my father and guru to an entire generation of princes – wasn't to raise a generation of mercenaries and suicide squads.

To everyone who came to his fold, Dron asked the same question.
Why are you here?
To be a hero.
To be the best archer ever!
To be the best wrestler.
Me too.
No shortage of world conquerors, I see. How about you show me if you can stand upright?

When we walked into the gurukul, an imaginary plumb line was dropped from the top of our cranium to the centre point on the ground between our feet. For the rest of our living days, we were accountable to that plumb line.
Too much weight on one leg. Too much lefty tilt.
Our spine was to be a sceptre planted in the earth. Dron would accept no less.

Astras are manipulated by sound as much as by thought and movement. The sonic landscape in a gurukul is very particular. Once a body has been reined in, it follows that sounds begin to matter: what the sounds mean and also, how they are articulated. No sound is to be uselessly deployed.
Just how deep down does your voice rise from? Nose? Throat? Chest? Belly?
Don't let words slop out of one side of your mouth.

We became aware of deeply ingrained asymmetry. Mortals are like upside-down trees whose roots draw sustenance from above, whose fruits ripen in soil. So many analogies are tree analogies.
With your posture, you reveal yourself. Easy, but not floppy. Alert, but not constipated.
Where we could, we were to aim for symmetry. Where there was no symmetry, we were to be artists of mindful movement and economy. Wave of arm began in the armpit and ended at fingertip, and every cell en route was accountable.

For what seemed like forever to a bunch of restless boys, we weren't so much as allowed to cut the air with a stick, let alone fight one another with swords. Instead we were taught to cook, clean, serve, mend and sew.
Without the wherewithal and courage to bring down a large animal in single combat, you have no business eating it!
We learned the shaastras, and how to make objects of wood, stone, clay, hemp. We climbed, swam, foraged for food in different seasons and settings.

So that we could treat a wound as effectively as we would someday inflict one, we were taught poultices, tinctures, the minds and hearts of herbs.
Pay attention! After years of being here, if a fool still dies eating a poisonous berry, I'd say he deserves his fate.
We learned about sacred geometry and sweet pentagrams, the frankness of flowers announcing their uncoy intent to the eyes of butterflies and bees.

Did that mean the gurukul raised a battalion of superheroes? Hardly. We were boys, not automatons. Most paid scant attention to anything but lessons about sharp projectiles and minor poisons. We were interested in burr that fastened in hair, stalks that became darts, leaves that caused frantic itching, leaves that made itching subside, mushrooms that made the sky explode into kaleidoscopic colours, leaves that turned teeth yellow, fruit that made teeth fall out, sly footbaths that made people wet their beds in sleep.

Elixirs and poisons were as important to my father as fighting strategy and arms. I knew my herbs well, not because of undue effort on my part, but from osmosis.

This gen (not weapons or mantras) is what has kept me intact over the millennia. A chiranjeevi's body isn't exempt from decay. Only those who have drunk amrit can escape that fate.

STRAIGHT, FLEXIBLE ARROW SHAFT

Eventually we got the swords, maces, bows and arrows we were waiting for.
Your target is that wooden bird. Before letting loose any arrow, tell me what you see.
Cloudy sky, outline of mountains and trees –
Langoors shaking the trees –
Wooden bird target tied to the branch –

I can see only the bird's left eye.
Step back, the rest of you. Arjun, step forth.
Song that is embedded in an archer's blood: Feet planted firm. Knees straight. Body steady and relaxed. Set the bow up with both hands. Nock the arrow. Close the fist, no gaps between fingers. Stretch the neck. Close mouth and eye. Unclench the jaw. Take aim. Smile at the thought of piercing your mark. Now let fly.

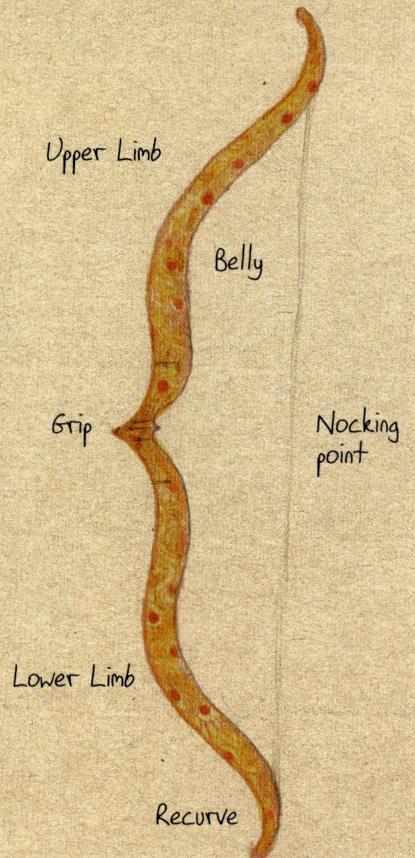


The hierarchy is simple: there are the archers; and then there are the rest. The rest thump one another in sweaty, brutish one-to-one combat, an archer operates from afar: clean, remote. His bow is sleek, his arrows strategic and sharp. A hundred foot soldiers can be staved off by a single man's quiver. Other warriors flex, clench. A relaxed archer is god on earth.

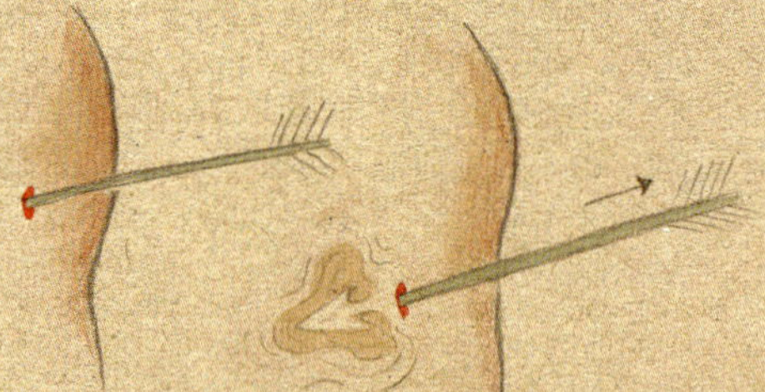

You cannot gouge out an arrowhead without taking out a hunk of flesh with it.

A curved piece of wood can dream of being a weapon if it is blunt and heavy enough to cause a concussion. What it can never be is an effective arrow. An arrow with a flawless, straight – and bendable – shaft is the only sort that can reliably meet its mark. Arjun was the straightest, most flexible arrow in my father's quiver. Not only was his body honed to symmetry in action and repose, he was also ambidextrous. I couldn't take my eyes off him, and I resented him profoundly.

Bali kept Indra on his toes. Asurs keep the devas from lapsing into hedonistic stupor. The arch foe is more useful to one's growth than a zombie acolyte, but who will explain that to the young? I wasted away, made myself sick with jealousy, hoping to catch my father's eye.
Had he not walked off with my father's heart so easily, had we been one generation apart or in different gurukuls, I could have admired Arjun openly, loved him even. I would have been spared the burn of being the rival he barely noticed. Unrequited resentment is far worse than unreturned love.

Why aren't you asleep yet?
Why won't you teach me what you teach him?
You aren't good enough! And that role isn't yours to play.
Don't let your heart shrivel, son. What lies ahead of Arjun isn't to be envied.
I was enjoying my cosy bog of self-pity too much to hear what he said.

To be a classic hero, you need a visible wound. It was easy to dislike Arjun because he had none. We will put up with cocky bastards as long as they have a visible wound. One little flaw that will allow us to temper our admiration with pity or disdain. Arjun wasn't quite hero material like Duryodhan or Karn.

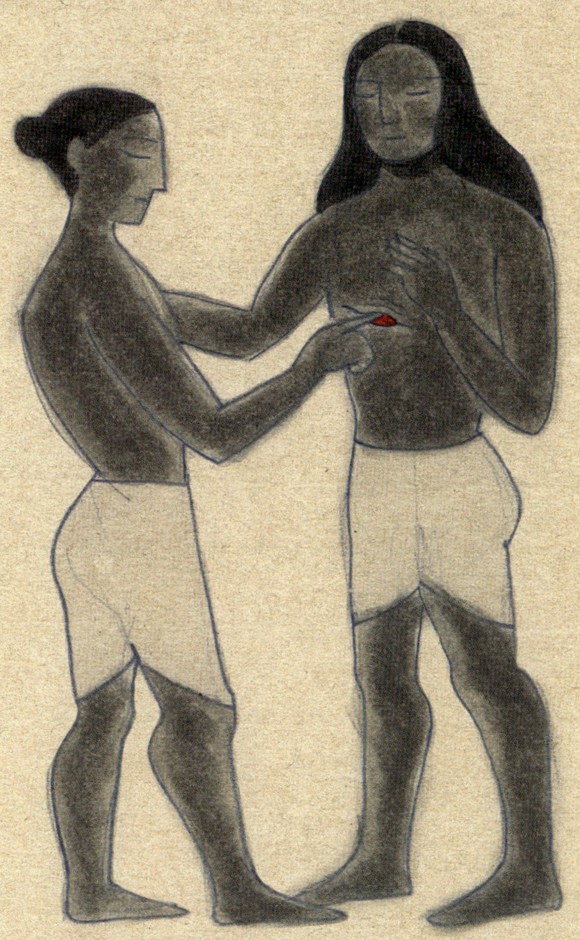

A heroic being without a visible wound evokes resentment, not love.

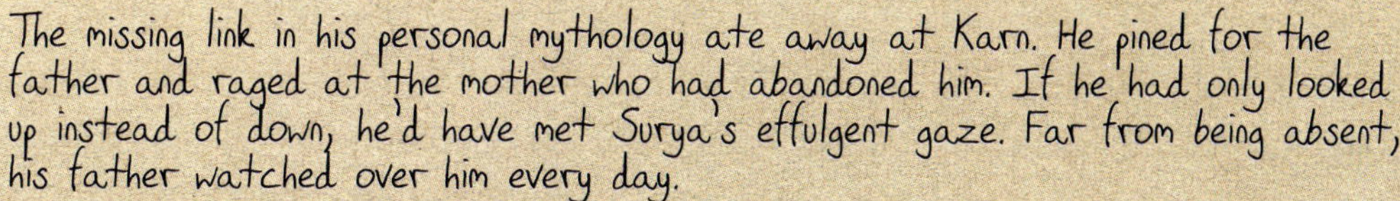

The missing link in his personal mythology ate away at Karn. He pined for the father and raged at the mother who had abandoned him. If he had only looked up instead of down, he'd have met Surya's effulgent gaze. Far from being absent, his father watched over him every day.

Despite what he said, I saw my father come up with tasks that put Arjun at a disadvantage so that I could catch up. He was given the leakier pail, heavier load, longer route. Even with those, Arjun could not be held back long.
A storm blew out all the lamps one new moon night. Arjun carried on – washed up, ate, practised his lessons – in darkness, as if nothing had happened. Led only by sound, he shot an arrow into the darkness and found his mark.

A fraction of existence is bathed in light. The rest is a dark place. Outside the paleness of suns, the universe is dark. The womb is dark. Trees have their roots in darkness. The body carries out repair and healing at night.

Points of light pose a threat more frequently than swatches of darkness. In too much light, the brain dulls, eyes barely stay open. To overemphasize light is to keep people stupid. There is power in befriending the dark.

I will make you the best archer this land has known.
As your gurudakshina, you will capture King Drupad in combat one day.

Three boys tried to challenge Arjun's bid to be the best archer. All vied for Dron's attention: I, Ashwatthama; Eklavya of the forest-dwelling Nishad tribe; and Karn, half-brother of the Pandavs, who hated Arjun even more than I did. (No one likes a teacher's pet, but being the object of a teacher's affection isn't half bad!)

Solar sons always run the risk of being singed.

Karn was the sun's own son. He had natural immunity that protected him from malignant forces without. But what was to save him from the malignant forces within? Their names are still uttered in hyphenation: Karn-Arjun. Both chose archery as their calling. They shared a resentment-fuelled magnetism. Arjun's biological father was as absent as Karn's. The absentee father left no scar tissue on Arjun. Karn, on the other hand, was marked for life by doubts about his identity.

As a little boy he gave his clothes away to the poor, came home naked. As a teenager he gave away the jewels he had. As a young man, if someone asked for his loyalty and heart – he gave both, unstintingly. He had no desire to hoard anything for himself. With the same fecklessness he viewed all material things with, Karn peeled off his golden armour and gave it away to the first person who asked.

Will the golden one give this beggar any alms?

From what I have, ask for what you will.

He was always peeling his skin to check what lay under. The person who asked for the armour was Indra, Arjun's biological father. He didn't ask out of any loyalty to his son, but out of longstanding enmity with Karn's father, Surya.

# SWORD KEEPS SWORD IN SHEATH

Karn sought solace in power. He pleaded to Dron for instruction and the Pashupat astra. My father asked him the same question he asked anyone who came to his door: Why are you here? Why do you crave power? Karn had no good response. Dron, never a fan of ambition in the self-aggrandizing, refused to be his teacher.

Karn decided to seek out a guru to surpass Dron. Who better than the volatile Parshuram, the man who gave Dron his most powerful astras? Parshuram's mission had been to cull the world of as many rajanyas as he could. His rationale for making my father heir to the astras was simple: my brahmin father would be guru to rajanyas on both sides of a war. He would make deadly warriors of the princes; and these armed monkeys could be let loose to destroy each other.

Karn feared his hazy natal story would be an obstacle for the rajanya-hating Parshuram. 'I do not know who I am, I come to you blank' would have been the right place to begin the rapport. Karn began with a lie instead.
Who are you?
An orphan from the same clan as you.
Parshuram took him in. Years went by. Karn was intuitive, well-mannered and prodigiously gifted. His teacher grew to love him dearly, though he knew the details in Karn's life story didn't add up. Instead of prying the truth out, Parshuram allowed it to reveal itself, as truths tend to do.

The day had been arduous. Karn offered his guru his lap to rest his head on. Being given the Pashupat seemed only a matter of time now. A flesh-boring worm snagged itself on Karn's thigh just as Parshuram fell into sleep.
Blood soaked through Karn's clothes.
Only a rajanya could endure so much pain.
You lied about who you are. Reveal yourself!

I always thought of you as a father. That's why I said your clan was mine.
Nonsense! You lied because you thought you couldn't get the Pashupat from me any other way.
What you've got from me will stay with you – but only until you enter your biggest battle.
And there your teacher's blessing will abandon you.
Karn, Eklavya and I. The curse of incomplete knowledge afflicted us all. All of us insisted on validation that our teachers, for this reason or that, were unwilling to supply. Malaise of the gifted who are in a hurry.

Eklavya was the wildcard. He walked into the ashram gates, a slip of a lad, demanding my father make him the best archer the world had known.
Why do you want to be that?
Because I CAN be that. And you are the only one who can make me that.
All hubris. Go away.
Some years later, in the forest:
Wow! Just take a look at this!
The muzzle of arrows was so skilful, it silenced the beast without so much as leaving a scratch. Dron didn't need to see Eklavya to recognize his work.

Who's your guru?
You! I prayed every day that you watch over my sadhana.
With cowrie eyes, I installed your spirit in a mound of clay. Then years, years of tapasya.

If I'm your guru and you've become so good, don't you owe me gurudakshina? I'd like to have your right thumb.
Anything you want, beloved one.
That he got as good as he did – better than any of us – with only a pair of cowrie eyes watching over him, is proof of the nishad's staggering talent.

In what seems like impossible brutality, a knowing gardener can hack half a tree down and ensure it grows back healthier next year. A gardener of idiot compassion sighs, 'Poor insect, poor weed' and ends up keeping neither bush nor vegetable plot alive. Can't handle culling? Be prepared for the grove to grow into a tangled, impenetrable thicket. The culling will still happen, but on the forest's terms. You will have outsourced brutality.

My father's methodology would find no favour in a free-particle favouring world. Too severe. Not egalitarian enough. Egalitarianism is a beautiful daydream. Show me an egalitarian jungle and I will show you a fox in a lion suit.

Contrary to the current narrative, Eklavya wasn't punished for being a poor forest boy with super skills. He was punished for a serious error: laying claim to a lineage he had done no ground-time to earn, from a teacher who had explicitly rejected him. Was Dron's rejection unjust? Arguably. I cannot justify my father's actions. But I do know the gurukul was a private one, where students were being honed for a mission. It owed Eklavya – or for that matter, Karn – nothing.

Karn and Eklavya should've just rejected elitist lineages; declared themselves to be what they were – swayambhus, self-actualised ones. That would've taken some audacity and courage. Ultimate cocking-a-snook at a system that kept them out.

So Eklavya conveniently disappeared from the tale.
Disappeared? No. He lived a fruitful life away from the din for a while –
Fruitful thumbless life for the archer-karmayogi! Long and short of the Eklavya story: your father was an asshole.
I'm your sutradhaar, but I'm still a product of my context and time, marked by attendant blindspots even though I try to be watchful. You aren't held hostage by old narratives. Re-story the shabby stories.

Threaded needle dips and surfaces. The stitches are fine, the embroidery more complex than would suit a simplistic eye. Eklavya never stopped being an archer. Dron's lineage nocked an arrow with the thumb; Eklavya's lineage shoots an arrow without using the thumb at all.
Eklavya fell out of the popular narrative with the thumb-slicing episode. But his story does not end there. Krshn's uncle Kamsa, tyrant king of Mathura, employed the thumbless archer as his general. Eklavya met his death at the hands of Krshn while attempting to wipe out Krshn's clan.

The forest tribe continued to hold a grudge against Krshn right until the day a nishad hunter shot a poisoned arrow into Krshn's right toe.
The avatar left his mortal coil on a forest floor. Balance will be restored, some say, and even an avatar isn't exempt. Others say the nishad hunter wept inconsolably at Krshn's side. His arrow had been meant for a deer.

Arjun got the Pashupat astra from Shiv in a dream transmission some years later. Dron gave the astra, unwillingly, to just one of his disciples: me.
From now on, no weapon will be necessary. In your hand, even a grass blade will be deadly.
Let your reasons for invoking the Pashupat never be trivial. Against a superhuman enemy, it will never fail you –
Aim it at a mortal and the astra will destroy the world as you know it.

Our days in the gurukul ended. From my father, the Kuru princes and I learned how to fight skilfully with clubs, swords, spears, javelins, lances. We learned to fight fully armoured and disarmed, mounted or on foot. Not everyone rose to excellence, but everyone learned how to face their own mortality. When the time of reckoning came on Kurukshetra, it could never be said that a student of Dron met death gracelessly.

I bullied my father with my tears, and his most serious breach of responsibility was giving me what I wanted. I wanted the Pashupat, his most valuable astra. So great was my hurry to master the mantra to invoke the Pashupat, I paid no attention to the antidote, the mantra to revoke the weapon.

There are fools in every generation who clamour for powers they aren't equipped to handle. There are irresponsible beings in every generation who enable such fools. The gods do not always have to devise complicated ways to bring you down. Sometimes it suffices to hand a monkey the machete he is angling for.
Sit back and watch him behead himself.

Would you be terribly offended if I laughed?
No. Go ahead.

The Pashupat wasn't the only oversized thing I insisted on. To swap astras is a mark of love and loyalty. Krshn was known to be generous with anyone who sought his help, so I decided to meet him one-on-one in Dwarka.
Can we trade my Pashupat for your Sudarshan Chakra?
But why do you want it?
Arjun has every astra I have. I really want something he hasn't got.
Today I touch my neck and marvel that my head still sits on it after such insolence. Maybe Krshn was amused by my childishness. He smiled.

Vishnu's little finger had once rested upon a petulant Garud's shoulder and crushed him to the ground. The weight of the Sudarshan was like that.
I love Arjun more than I love my own flesh. But he has never made such a demand of me. Take the chakra if you must.
Take this thing back! It's too intense! My skin is melting off me!
He didn't behead me that day. Nor later, when he took my jewel away. After millennia of sleepless wandering, I regret not having been decimated by the 108 serrations of the Sudarshan so I could fuse with Krshn's body and sleep.

I saw that strange melting phenomenon again at Yudhishthir's coronation. Krshn beheaded his cousin Shishupal with the Sudarshan. Particles of what had been Shishupal rose, then fused into Krshn completely, like water beads into the ocean.

Is the Sudarshan Chakra best shown as a jagged flying disc or as a mathematical sequence or as a moustached minor divinity armed to the teeth? Is Krshn best shown as a galactic nursery? Or a dirt-eating blue baby? Or a dark, bejewelled androgyne? Is devlok – antithesis of dense, low-frequency matter – best shown as purple-pink mountains or as a blank page? All these diagrams – crude as their executor – are only my attempts at making Enormous accessible.

# HOUSE ON FIRE

The citizens of Hastinapur didn't dislike Duryodhan – he was an able prince, a generous friend – they just liked the Pandavs more. Duryodhan's undoing, like mine, was his insecurity. His father, like mine, walked a continuous tightrope between the desire to play fair and the desire to see his son thrive.
If you let this happen again, I will kill myself.
Calm down, boy.
Bheem shook us off the tree, into the Yamuna! The current was so strong, we could have drowned! Do you care at all?
The swaggering, leery image of Duryodhan that lingers posthumously confuses me. The Duryodhan I knew was incredibly fragile. He had a hard time staying put in his skin. The Pandavs – Bheem in particular – blistered his sanity.

Born on the same day of the same year, Bheem and Duryodhan were identical of build, matching in force. They had the Karn-Arjun variety of twinny hostility. Each chose mace combat and freestyle wrestling as their preferred forms.
In the akhada, it was hard to tell them apart -
Symmetrical as an inkblot folded in half. The difference was that Bheem was guileless as summer, while Duryodhan rumbled with conspiracy and paranoia like a stormy sky. The rivalry began as regular boyhood rough-and-tumble. But it wasn't long before a dangerous edge crept into Duryodhan's plots.

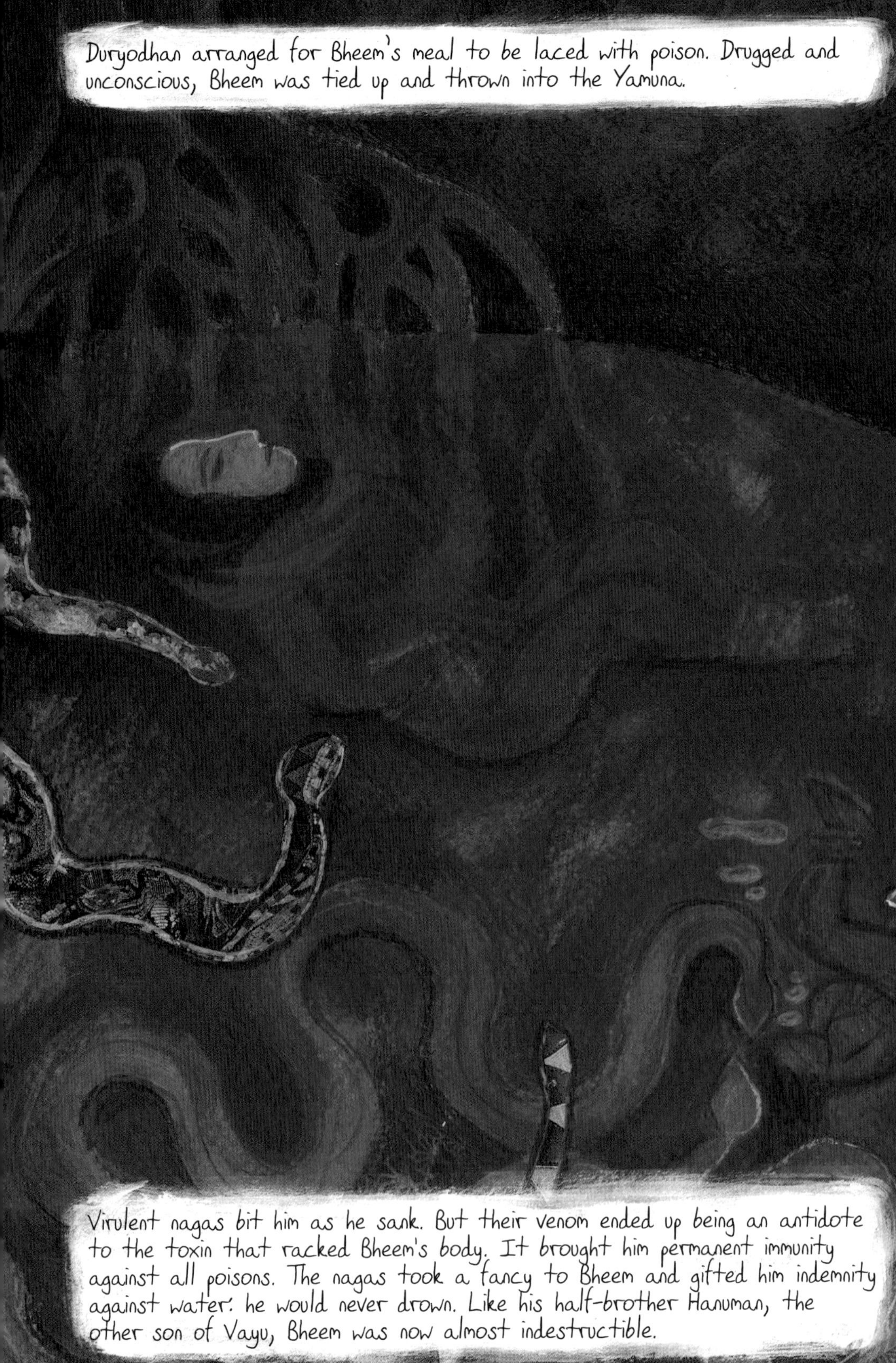
Duryodhan arranged for Bheem's meal to be laced with poison. Drugged and unconscious, Bheem was tied up and thrown into the Yamuna.
Virulent nagas bit him as he sank. But their venom ended up being an antidote to the toxin that racked Bheem's body. It brought him permanent immunity against all poisons. The nagas took a fancy to Bheem and gifted him indemnity against water: he would never drown. Like his half-brother Hanuman, the other son of Vayu, Bheem was now almost indestructible.

Then came the episode of the burning house. At Duryodhan's insistence, his unseeing father invited the Pandavs to an out-of-town idyll. The lovely house they stayed in, though, had been coated with highly inflammable shellac and was set afire in the dead of night.
The Pandavs had been tipped off about this assassination plan by their uncle Vidur. Five unsuspecting forest-dwellers and their mother were sent to a fiery death – decoy corpses to trick the Kauravs while the Pandavs escaped into the forest. The injustices heaped on forest-dwellers would keep mounting.

The trees and underbrush have kept me company longer than people have. As the forests grow scantier in the world around me, they grow denser in my narrative. It is easy for me to slip into metaphors of the forest.
If Duryodhan was a tree of dark passions, Dhritrashtra was its roots; Karn, its trunk; Shakuni, its branches; the Kaurav siblings, its flowers and fruit. If Yudhishthir was a tree of righteousness, Krshn was its roots; Arjun, its trunk; Bheem, its branches; the twins, its flowers and fruit.

Hastinapur wasn't safe for the Pandavs until they had gathered strength and allies, grown in strategic wisdom. Their forest years gave them time for that. No one is consistently glorious. Some people never get a chance to play the lead role on stage. Those who do, often spend years rehearsing that one entry and hope they don't blow their line. The years right after the burning house episode were Bheem Years. He kept his brothers and mother safe and in good spirits. When they were disheartened or exhausted, Bheem's shoulders were their wings.

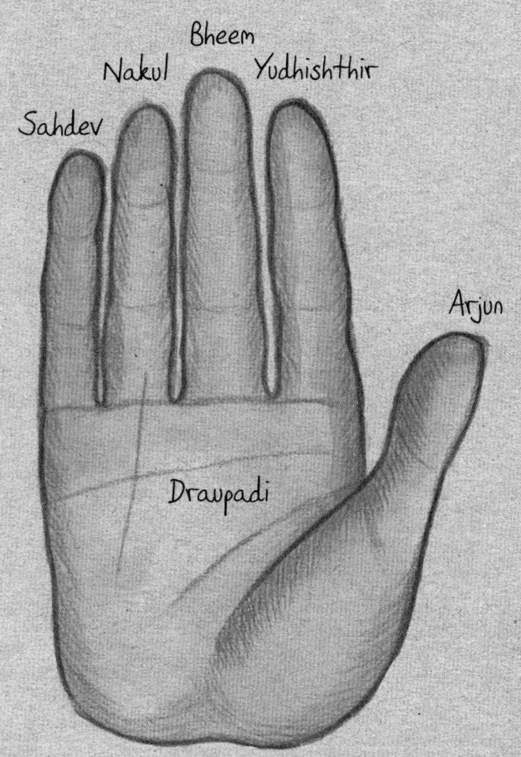


The analogy of the hand is a useful one. Yudhishthir: forefinger, ether, monarch. Bheem: middle finger, air, wall to guard the monarch. Arjun: thumb, worth more than half the hand, natural ally of the forefinger. Nakul: ring finger, sun and moon, fed directly by the artery connected to the heart. Sahdev: little finger, ruled by earth, baby of the family, beloved of all. An open fist is reassurance, charity, peace. A closed fist: forces united, makeshift hammer, war.

The uncomplicated meritocracy of the forest suited Bheem very well. He met Hidimba, from a tribe of forest-dwelling rakshasas, when he killed her tyrant brother. She was stricken, and pursued him the only way she knew: directly.
You big, sexy man. Be mine!
He would make a devoted husband to Draupadi one day, but it was voluptuous Hidimba who was Bheem's true companion, his soul friend and love.

In their simplicity, strength and appetite for life, Bheem and Hidimba were matched. She taught him the secrets of her people, became the mother of his child. The Pandavs and Pritha approved of the union, but everyone knew it could not last. The Pandavs' destiny lay outside the forest.
Outside the forest Hidimba would have pined away.

The asur Baka

After their year among the rakshasas, the Pandavs took refuge with a poor brahmin family in Ekachakra. They were hospitable and discreet, but the Pandavs soon learned they had a secret sadness.

An asur named Baka lived on the fringes of the village. He demanded a cartload of rice and a human every week so he wouldn't lay waste to the village. The sacrificing family was chosen by lots, and it was now the turn of the Pandavs' hosts.

At night, the host family argued about who ought to be sent to Bakasur. Each member insisted on being the sacrificial offering – none more vehemently than the baby of the family. He said he ought to go, since he didn't know life well enough to miss it.

That boy made me think of a family of saranga birds trapped in the Khandav inferno. The newborns were being raised by their mother, since their father had deserted the nest to be with another female. The mother bird was in a panic.
I can't possibly carry you all to safety! Who do I save? Who gets left behind? How can a mother choose?
Should I just hide you in a rat hole?
No! We'd rather go up in flames than be eaten alive slowly by rats!
Save your own life, Mother! We are so little and useless!

You've suffered enough, holding it together all alone. You're still young, Mother. Find a new mate, make a new family.
If he sees us all alone, Agni may even take pity on us and spare our lives.
Crazed by helplessness, the mother flew away. Agni didn't let the babies burn.

Bheem stepped in and announced that he would go as sacrificial food for Baka. After an animated battle, Bakasur was slain. Had someone from the brahmin's household been devoured by Baka, the family would never have been in the mood to share trivia about Krshna Draupadi's swayamvar, Arjun would never have made it there in time to win over their wife. There would have been no powerful alliance with the Panchals, the Pandavs wouldn't have been transformed by meeting Krshn, and Karn would likeliest have won Draupadi's hand.

Only a fool would try to trace every tempest back to a seagull, but some flapping seagull wings have surely led to tempests on the other side of the world.

Once the Pandavs left Ekachakra, it was Arjun who took a torch and led the way. He left the wings, entered the proscenium, took Bheem's place. He would be their protector now.

# BURNISHED GOLD TRIANGLE

Even those who swore their hungers were well looked after wanted Draupadi. Everyone who was someone tried to win her at the swayamvar. She was vocal, though about what she didn't care for. Many fragile egos were shattered.
Looking at its reflection, put an arrow through the target above. Do this, and my sister will see if she likes you enough.
I know the bearded man. It's the Pandav, Arjun!
Drupad immediately recognized Arjun from the gurudakshina-capturing. Giveaway bowstring scars of the ambidextrous archer – on both shoulders, not one.

In the gathered audience, Krshn recognized the Pandavs too. Drupad signalled his delight and his approval of Arjun to Draupadi. It wasn't really necessary.
The swayamvar is over. I have chosen my mate.
Draupadi's eyes are perfectly symmetrical, like lotus petals –
Krshna Draupadi's hair is blue-black as rain-bearing clouds.
The wilful, golden Krshna Draupadi had already locked eyes with Arjun. She was shot through with more love arrows than the moving target above him.

She had plummeted to her death in the high mountains thousands of years ago. In public memory, Draupadi remains recorded in obsessive detail, as if we set eyes on her yesterday. The deep valley between her breasts, her smell –
Her thighs tapering like plantain stems.
Her body glistening with sweat that brings to mind jasmines on a hot summer night.
All analogies – even those of flame, rose and ruby – were inadequate.

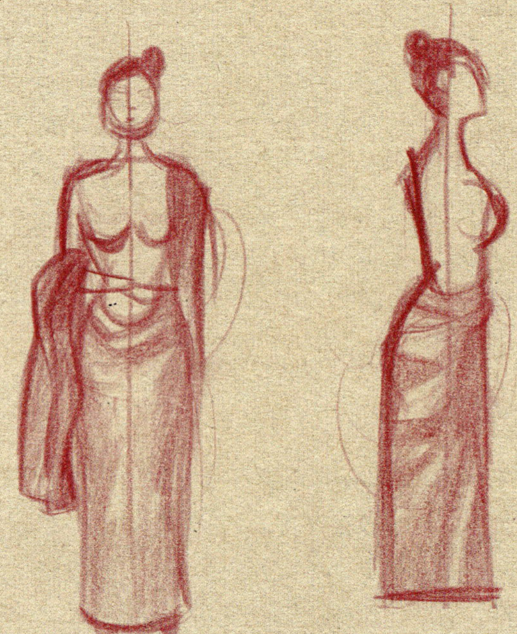

From looking at her I learned that 'regal' has nothing to do with 'beautiful'. Draupadi was queen without ever needing to be crowned one. Regal has a spinal cord quality. Other epithets – pretty, gamine, effervescent, languid, smouldering, sexy – do not have that spinal cord quality. In movement, regal comes from a delicately caliberated play of stemmy uprightness and grace. In drape, regal is the ability to pull off sinuousness from within wrapped yards of fabric.

That swayamvar punctured a lot of kings with scintillae of unfulfilment. It was involuntary. To know Draupadi was to want her, and be pierced by the realization that she was not in your league, that you would permanently burn with longing.

Arjun won Draupadi over at the swayamvar, but his brothers were desperately in love with her too. And then, because she was no ordinary woman, because her rules were her own, Draupadi chose to embrace them all.

You're not going to slide by with that! I've heard this story told quite differently.

Not what I've heard either. I heard she was tricked into being their common wife!

No one's returning from the dead to tell us what really happened, but a woman who took lip from no one could hardly be yoked to a post like a lamb –

There was nothing common about that 'common wife'.

Keep aside moral knee-jerk and the need to proclaim Draupadi victim. She was amshavtar not of one goddess but many. Between the five brothers, they had most virtues covered, and were beautiful in myriad physical ways.
Draupadi seems to have had her men on her terms – a year with each, during which she would not be disturbed by any of the others. The hard part wasn't mating with five lovely men. (The hard part came later: of feeling bereft in a crowd.) By all accounts, the newly-weds were blissful in those early years.

She was like Gaja Lakshmi anointed by five elephants. Pritha was hardly a prude about this – she saw the merits of her sons united by Draupadi's fire.
The only consent you must seek is hers. Your marriage needs no other approval.
The Pandavs took other wives and lovers in the course of their lives. But the sun of the house, the central yagna fire, was unquestionably Draupadi. Doomed hour in the gaming hall aside, they treated her like a jewel.

Their atypical marriage might make sense given the circumstance of how the Pandavs landed up in mrityulok. Irritated by Indra Purandara's hubris, Shiv sent him to face the true extent of his originality and uniqueness.

You are quite insufferable. I banish you to the high mountains.

I will be the first to plant my flag on the highest peak.

Even in adversity, Purandara's cocky ambitiousness remained intact.

His plan proved to be hardly original: the high peaks were littered with flags planted by countless Indras bygone. Ashamed, Purandara hid in a cave. But he wasn't alone there either. Four other Indras, equally skilled and handsome, gave him company – all banished by Shiv for being insufferable.
Off to mrityulok! Subdue your vanity and remain united, then you may return.
Born in mrityulok as the Pandavs, the Indras sought fire to fuse them all together. They would never be separated by the rivalries and whims of spouses.

Many things fell into place the day the Pandavs united with Draupadi. They met their cousin Krshn for the first time. Krshn was Narayan incarnate. Where there is Narayan, there Narad must be – singing hermit ferrying word and warning between worlds. There, too, must Nara be – Narayan's loyal human counterpart. In that epoch, Arjun was Nara to Krshn's Narayan.
At Draupadi's swayamvar, the burnished gold triangle locked complete.

A celibate offering conjugal advice is rich in irony, but it was Narad who told the Pandavs how to divide time with Draupadi so they wouldn't disembowel each other like Sunda and Upasunda did. Life had been a continuous high-five for the asur twins. They were inseparable, devoted, they ruled their empire in unison.
Sunda
Upasunda
Until Tilottama came along.

Indra, unsettled by the twins' might, sent her to eliminate the brothers. She was bewitching, Tilottama, with moles in the forms of constellations; and she was the only thing Sunda and Upasunda could not agree about.
Both fell in love with her. Each wanted her for himself, exclusively. Brothers who would've gladly given their lives for one another, ended up taking each other's life over Tilottama. Job done, the apsara returned to devlok.

# FIRE TETRAHEDRON

I've seen fires for too long and from too close to think of them as erratic, illogical entities. Fires are predictable because they are demanding. No fire ever lived without stringent enablers: oxygen, heat, fuel. And a chain reaction to keep the dance going. Take one enabler away and the fire cannot live. So it is with all fires: whether terrestrial, submarine, or in the digestive tract.

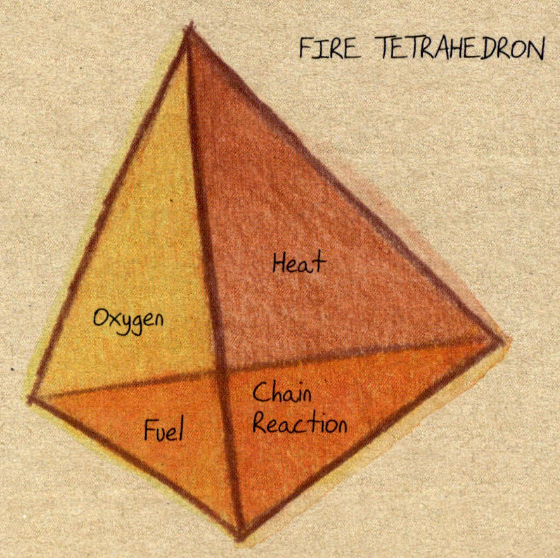


Backed by a powerful spouse, a mighty father-in-law and a wise friend, the Pandavs emerged from their exile. Dhritrashtra mumbled sounds of welcome. They were sheepishly gifted a tract of forested land called Khandav-van, away from Hastinapur, to set up their own capital.

If throngs of fools must live in some sort of order – with no clue how to work the land – a forest must burn. The first thing Krshn-Arjun did to sound their union as Narayan-Nara of our times, was burn down a primeval forest. Burning the forest widened the chasm between city-dwellers and forest-dwelling tribes.

Small fires in a big forest keep flammable matter in check. A periodic purge may prevent a large-scale catastrophe. Useful, where civilization is concerned.
A forest with sentimental guards – where no twig is plucked, no underbrush culled, dry leaves left to pile high – will blaze into an inferno with scintillae of summer. Nature can handle this all right. Human settlements, not so well.

The Khandav carnage was one of the most brutal in history.
Is there no gentler way to get this done?

Of course! Forget about Hastinapur, forget family history. Continue to live as nomads and seekers!
But if it's empire you want, forest must burn!
They waited at opposite ends and massacred all that escaped the fire.

A boy isn't a man until he holds his own against a powerful father, or kills him. Indra wanted to protect his naga friends in the forest. He thundered down upon his son Arjun. Cables of lightning and big boulders fell from the sky. Arjun fought them off alone.

I'll fight you again but, damn, you're good. Let me do something nice for you.

I like me a story where a person concedes defeat not just with grace, but with generosity as well. Low-grade players see sycophancy where there is magnanimity. High-grade players are confident enough to give opponents their due. Indra promised to give Arjun astras when the time was right for him to receive them.

Several causes unite in one effect. Suffice to say, Khandav-van had to burn. The city raised atop charred birds, animals, trees and forest-dwellers was called Indraprasth, after the rain god who tried to guard the forest in vain. Everything about Indraprasth was illusory and unsustainable. Even its architect was the asur Maya. Illusion.
Those without a genuine connection to the elements are always besotted by Mayasur's confections. They prefer shimmering artifice to the muted palette and mud clumps a forest floor yields.
For all Maya's efforts, Indraprasth would be inhabited only fleetingly. The desert crept in at its hemlines, waiting to lay claim.

A good fight is no more innocent or unbloody than any other kind of fight.
Did they know? The Pandavs gearing up for the good fight?

The Pandavs acknowledged the place of Krshn in their lives fully and publicly at Yudhishthir's coronation. They chose elder over older, cowherd over king, merit over protocol, and offered arghya* to Krshn first. This hurt a lot of gathered people; though, tellingly, the other most deserving candidates – Bheeshm, Vidur, Vyas – did not mind the choice.

Heart of the passiflora flower reminds me of the Pandav sanctum: axis-centre Krshn with the five Pandavs in a loving circle around him.

Krshn's cousin Shishupal of Chhedi protested the loudest, and most convincingly. It is understandable that Shishupal wasn't crazy about Krshn. Krshn had killed people Shishupal loved and made away with his bride Rukmini. Everyone is a victim in their own narrative.

* Libation to gods, rishis, Elders

When Krshn's cousin Shishupal was born, his attributes were oddly Vishnu-esque. But the little mutant tended towards dissonance and had a strong aversion to his cousin, obvious the moment he was first set in Krshn's lap.
Why does he bawl like this? I get a bad feeling inside –
Is my boy meant to die at your hands? You won't do that to me, will you?
One hundred transgressions on his part I'll forgive. When he oversteps, he will still remain a part of me.
The tot screamed, his third eye withered and sank, his extra arms fell off.

One hundred transgressions had already been pardoned. Shishupal was full of vitriol when he opposed the arghya offering at Yudhisthir's coronation.
Is this immoral low life the best you can choose?
The Sudarshan lopped his head off perfectly. There was a moment of shocked silence, then great beauty as Shishupal's essence became a part of Krshn.

He opened the eyes of some, closed the eyes of others. But the pickings weren't random. What Krshn offered to one, he offered to all. Over and over, in different settings, we stubbornly refused to reach out. The Pandavs, on the other hand, chose to reach out. They sought Krshn's counsel while the Kauravs were still dismissing him as an upstart. The rest of us ignored him until it was impossible to do so any longer.

Directly beneath
the lamp, darkness.

Have compassion for those too close to the trajectory of an outlier.
It's hard to recognize greatness in proximity. Harder still, to acknowledge it.
A rishi once observed that a prophet is recognized last in his own village.

To learn a queasy truth, ask yourself this:
Who's the Shiv to your Daksha?
Of the worthiest of worthies, whose name do you refuse to say aloud while a litany of others are mentioned? Who do you hesitate to leave room for in your crowded altar, though their credibility is immaculate?
Of the worthiest of worthies, who do you give thanks to?

For as long as folks could remember, an unhinged looking man had run around town pushing a wheel with a stick. He often wore no clothes, and his eyes had a glint like seers and madmen do. Children ran alongside him sometimes, pushing wheels of their own. Few others paid attention.
One day, out of indolence or inebriation or both, someone kicked the man in the gut, broke his stick in two, and sent the wheel wobbling off course.
The ground trembled, the world was shaken off its axis. The man turning his wheel had kept order intact, only no one knew. The greatest sages operate like this, in secrecy. Largesse under cover.

# HEART OF DICE

Everything about the Pandavs rankled Duryodhan. Their popularity, the splashy luxury of their capital designed by Maya, the master illusionist. Duryodhan had recurrent nightmares about his embarrassing visit to Indraprasth. He walked into a camouflaged door, he fell into a perfect ripple-free pool.
Draupadi saw his bumbling, threw her head back and broke into peals of laughter.
That sound! That sound!

Duryodhan's father, the king, oscillated between bitterness and guilt.
I beg of you, get rid of the Pandavs.
We have so much. There's enough to go around. Learn to share with your cousins.
Venomous serpents crawl underfoot, and my father suggests I walk barefoot.
I might as well destroy myself before the Pandavs manage to destroy me.
Dhritrashtra's old malice returned. He discussed the matter with his aides. He sought advice from all and sundry, never to heed a word. Father and son were like two anchorless boats harnessed together in a violent storm.

Dhritrashtra's dissuasions never lasted long enough to deter his son. And so Duryodhan set about making yet another destructive plan with his uncle Shakuni as counsel. They invited the Pandavs to a lavish new gaming hall in Hastinapur for a round of dice. A good king has no business gambling, but even near-flawless men have secret addictions. Yudhishthir loved games of chance, though he had neither mind nor flair to play them.

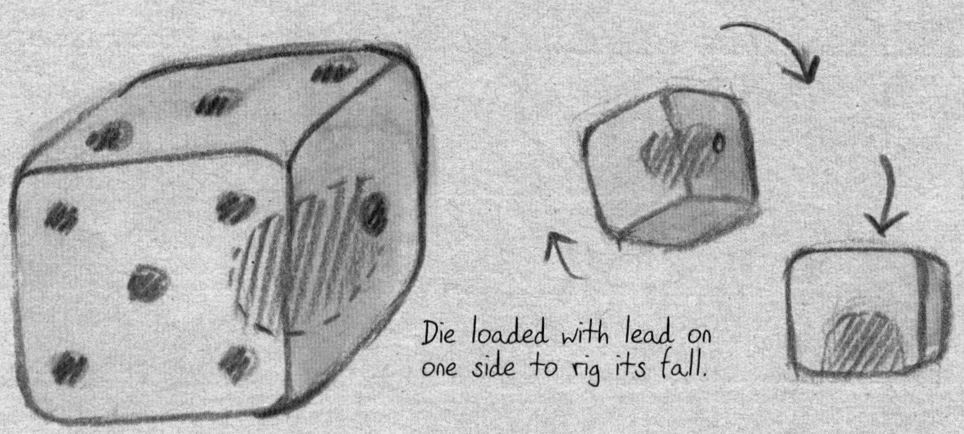


The terms were simple. Winner took all. Losers were exiled for twelve years and one. The Pandav king had lost before the game began. The dice were no ordinary dice, you see. Shakuni had loaded their hearts dark and heavy. The dice would fall only as he wanted them to.

During my continental drift, I reached a village whose inhabitants had begun to dance - hundreds of people, young and old, with no accompanying music or attendant reason. They danced compulsively, without any trace of joy.

They danced like that for weeks, unable to say why or stop, until they all fell in a heap and died of exhaustion. Indeed, the world is odd.

But this has happened over and over in myriad ways: cloud of unrecognizable behaviour engulfs the collective, brings on unmitigated madness. Our jaws drop, as if we couldn't have thought such a thing possible, but our history says we knew, we knew! We enable the madness that descends on us.

You lose.
You lose.
You lose.
You lose.
You lose.

stake my wealth.
I stake my armies and attendants.
I stake my brothers.
I stake myself.
I stake our peerless Draupadi.

Your foolish brother lost again! Messenger, go bring our slave girl, Draupadi.

O Queen. They summon you to the gaming hall.
She asked the messenger if a lost man had the right to stake anyone else.

Irked by the messenger's failure, Duryodhan sent his brother to get Draupadi.
You and I had no fight until this day, Dusshasan, but laying a finger on me will cost you very dearly.

He dragged her by her hair and blood-stained drape all the way to the hall.
We'll see about that.
You're hurting me!

She was cast there, dishevelled, her thundercloud hair in disarray. I have seen sacrificial animals treated with more gentleness. It became really hard to breathe in the gaming hall. The air seemed to have been sucked out of my lungs. The only loud voices were Karn and Duryodhan's.
These losers have nothing to offer you. Even the skin on their backs isn't their own!
You've chosen poorly, five times too often, but it isn't too late. Pick Karn. Or me. Real stallion for a fine mare.
Duryodhan bared his right thigh and slapped it in lascivious invitation. The daughter gets a man's left thigh; the right thigh is reserved for the lover.

Bheem swore to rip the thigh Duryodhan bared. He was the only one to plainly call out the madness that unfolded that day.
My favourite part – cranium pops like a coconut. Phat! Swaha!
You should've all been struck by lightning. for abetting a crime –
We WERE struck by lightning. Kauravs, Pandavs and all of us.

Vishwamitra rishi wanted to be Vashishth rishi's equal. Jealous of the older sage, he heckled him from the other side of the river. Vashishth waved away Vishwamitra's aggression with good humour, seeing his opponent's potential, but also his immaturity. Vishwamitra met the lovely Kamdhenu in Vashishth's land. The wish-granting cow was coveted by all, but she chose Vashishth.
How well you serve me! Leave this old git and be mine!
You overvalue yourself. You are just a guest. It's my rishi I serve.
Kamdhenu's bluntness irked Vishwamitra. He ensnared her.
Save me!
You are more powerful than I am. Gentle one, show him your wrath!

Anyone who dwells exclusively on the docility of cows does not recognize the nature of the animal at all. Kamdhenu was Bhoo Devi herself. Like the earth, she had a terrifying aspect AND a serene one.
Vishwamitra fell to the ground, begging for mercy.

Unbound will my hair remain, uncombed, until it is washed with your blood.
The stains on Draupadi's saree made her vulnerable. Her hair – so much of it! – gave her a particular, terrifying divinity.

Later narratives embellished the violence – stripping away her upper drape, having Draupadi crouch to hide her breasts, bringing metaphysical intervention in the form of bales of fabric – as if the fact of transgression needed to be made weightier. Hurting a single hair on Draupadi's head was transgression enough.
Elders, olders, courtiers, kin: you looked on in silence while I was humiliated. Hastinapur's knees have been broken.
What followed was a formality: spasms and kicking legs of an already beheaded goat.

They had harboured a persecution complex for so long, Duryodhan and Karn were unrepentant of their actions and words. They genuinely believed everyone else was wrong, and that they alone were right. Multiversal truth: On the brink of dissolution, perverse is the logic that prevails.
Clad in rags and ashes, the Pandavs went into forest exile for twelve years and one, each brother having sworn specific vengeance. Draupadi, lolling tongue that could lick every sanguine drop, said nothing at all.

Their first exile had been of flowering youth and acquisitions. They knew the forest opened into a clearing of pure possibility. The boys and Pritha travelled light, joined later by Draupadi and their counseller, the brahmin Dhaumya.
The second exile was different. They were older, pulses quick with foreboding. This time, the forest would only open into near-total annihilation.

Yudhisthir was not an underdog anymore. He was the defeated-but-beloved king. Thousands followed the Pandavs from the city to the edge of the forest.
You'll serve us best by returning to your lives.

The snatak brahmins and sages stayed on, the rest returned. Most evenings were spent sharing stories. History to know where they came from. Allegory to know where to go. Parable to keep the conscience crackling.

Don't deplete the forest or overgraze the land.

Or overstay your welcome.

Today I'm boiling the grain with some nettle leaves. Should be good.

The early years of exile were uncomplicated. Draupadi's hair grew matted and wild, but there were entire days when she did not revisit her rage. The royals lived in true companionship, tending to home and fire, hunting, cooking, sleeping with heavy stars above their bedrolls.

Sages pre-empted inevitable restlessness: what to do during an exile so long?
Travelling gives you time to learn, atone, still the busy mind.
There came a list of recommendations: energy-suffused tirthas and river unions to visit in different parts of the land. Some accessible, some arduous.
But there's no real need to go to the ends of the earth to do all that –

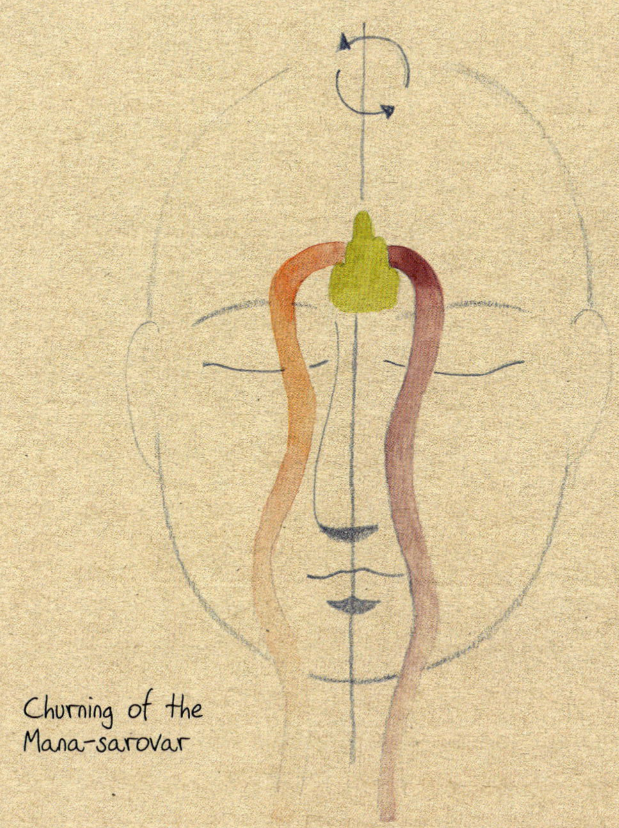

Churning of the Mana-sarovar

This is what the sages told the Pandavs as a quiet footnote: There's no need to haul your derriere from mountain to mountain, project to project, battle to battle. There are 108 tirthas, right here, in the human body. Living with attentiveness, one can learn from them all that the tirthas outside have to teach you.

People hear what they want to hear. The idea of sitting around observing the body with full attention for twelve years made Bheem and Arjun antsy. And so, the matter about bodily tirthas duly ignored, the Pandavs set off – sans entourage – to seek adventure, revelation and divine armaments.

A forest is many things to many people, but it is transformation above all. Krshna Draupadi and the Pandavs walked into the forest together, but really, it was five different forests they entered.

MANY FORESTS

Nakul and Sahdev's forest quickly opened out into a flower-laden meadow. These uncelebrated twins were the most resolved of the Pandavs.
They served, healed, listened. They brought nothing but sweetness to a setting where emotions were fraught, but heroic stories seldom valorize quiet sanity.

Yudhishthir's forest was the solitude of savant emperors. He yearned to understand the world rather than dominate it. To this end, he sought the company of itinerant sages who tested his sukshmata – as man, and as ruler.
Is a big sacrifice greater than a small sacrifice?
Whom to protect? Whom to deprive of their natural prey?
Is a raptor more virtuous or a serpent?
Is charity more vital or austerity?
I think your way isn't pacific, it's just cowardly –
His even temper and fair play earned him the love of strangers, but intimacy craves hot blood, not equanimity; a bias that tips in favour of the object of affection. No one was more agitated by his sangfroid than Draupadi.

He was tested by other-worldly creatures as well. Like the yaksha in guise of a crane, who guarded a magic lake. One Pandav after another went to drink its water and never returned. Yudhi found them lying in a death swoon.
Don't drink this water!
Answer my questions first, and I'll spare you and one brother of your choosing.
Ask, then. And if I must ask for the life of only one brother to be spared, spare one of the twins, so Madri's bloodline gets to survive as well.

Checking his overconfidence was Bheem's forest. To his chidlike heart, the forest was homecoming, not shadowland. He liked the simple pleasures and satisfying labour. Having figured out this wasn't Draupadi's favourite setting, he tended to her with utmost gentleness, scaled heights and took risks for something as innocuous as bringing her an armful of the lotuses she loved.
Move it, monkey. Out of my way!
I am old and weak. Can you lift my tail and place it where no one will trample on it?

'Can' I lift it, he asks! Ha ha!
With all force and all leverage he tried, but Bheem could not even budge the old beat-up looking monkey's tail. He apologized profusely.
I don't know what you are, but I am no match for you.
When you don't get too cocky, you're all right.
The langoor turned out to be his half-brother, Hanuman. Great was their joy.

Arjun's learning curve never waned, the hunger was always strongest in him. He chose to exit the hive and live out some of the exile solo. Walking in on Yudhishthir and Draupadi making love one night gave him a good alibi to leave.
So coy! Nothing here you haven't seen before, love.
With Narad as witness we vowed not to disrupt the intimate time of our brothers. I've failed.
So he left for a few years.
Then came the love affairs – those we know of, and all the encounters never recorded. With Ulupi, the naga princess, he played in nether worlds.

With Chitrangada, heir to the kingdom of Manipur, he had a son. They had to part because she would not abandon her responsibility to her land. The stormy chemistry with apsara Urvashi didn't end well. He backed off when he learned she had sexed one of his ancestors. That made her quite mad.
Are you being ageist or just stupid? I'm an apsara! The chronology and morals of men mean nothing to me.
She cursed him to a year of impotence for spurning her advances.

His quest for arms took him to places inaccessible to mortals. He met his father Indra for the first time after the Khandav-van combat. It was a fond reunion. Indra gave him special eyes to see the realms of divinity.

It's time for you to leave now. When you learn to dance and have Shiv's blessing, come back and take the astras you need.

They were hard tasks. Vishnu and Brahm respond to anyone who calls, even if they call by mistake. Shiv, however, must be won over – and flattery or charm don't work. Shiv is oblivious to everything but authenticity and effort.

Arjun did learn to dance, and it proved useful. In the last year of exile, he lived out Urvashi's curse in the guise of Brihanalla, the dancing hermaphrodite. To dance is to fuse male and female, solar and lunar; turn swagger to sway.
Krshn had danced Kaliya into submission; the gopis' love manifested as dance. Before the final act of the leela, Nar needed to dance like Narayan did.

Draupadi's forest could be impenetrably dark. The men who loved her with ardour weren't the ones she ached for; the men she loved most could belong only to the multitudes. In the moment of reckoning, she had felt abandoned by both.
Five protectors, but I remain defenceless.
I wanted Subhadra to have your blessing before she met anybody else.
Think of me as sister, not as rival-in-love.
Loverboy left on the pretext that he disturbed my dignity. He returns flaunting a new flame. On his terms must Draupadi offer benediction.

Her role as yagna fire eclipsed her other roles: she was Mother who barely
knew her sons and Queen who wasn't fated to enjoy the comforts of royalty.
Draupadi's forest was vengeance, even as she let the victim card go.

END GAME

You would think that after so many years of exile, the Pandavs would return to Hastinapur armed and vengeful. Instead, they asked Krshn to go as their peace envoy. It proved to be futile. Other than ceasing to exist, there was nothing the Pandavs could do to take Duryodhan's resentment away.
They ask for five villages, big or small. That is all.
Five villages! Dream on. I won't give up even a pinhead's measure of land.
Krshn's terms were predictably dismissed. Duryodhan could have relented, come out the bigger person. But he was torn by his own self-loathing, by an unseeing father's frustrations and a blindfolded mother's sense of being denied.

He brayed like a donkey when he was born. I was told to snuff him out to spare others.
Destiny is predisposition, it isn't written in stone. You can override yours if you make an effort.
Yeah yeah, blah blah. Who do you think you are? Why do we let a cowherd take up so much of our time?

I am This. And now that you know, Hastinapur, what will your next move be?
There was no move. Everyone froze, bathed in light: Vishwaroop as pearls before swine. The moment passed, blinding gloria disappeared from memory.

Where was the Pandavs' pride? A wise man knows better than to strut before a master or humble himself before fools.
What use were their divya astras?
It was not time for wrath – yet.

Some journeys make kill-kill Parshurams of people. Others make bemused Vishnus. We are conditioned to see the former as the solution to all problems.

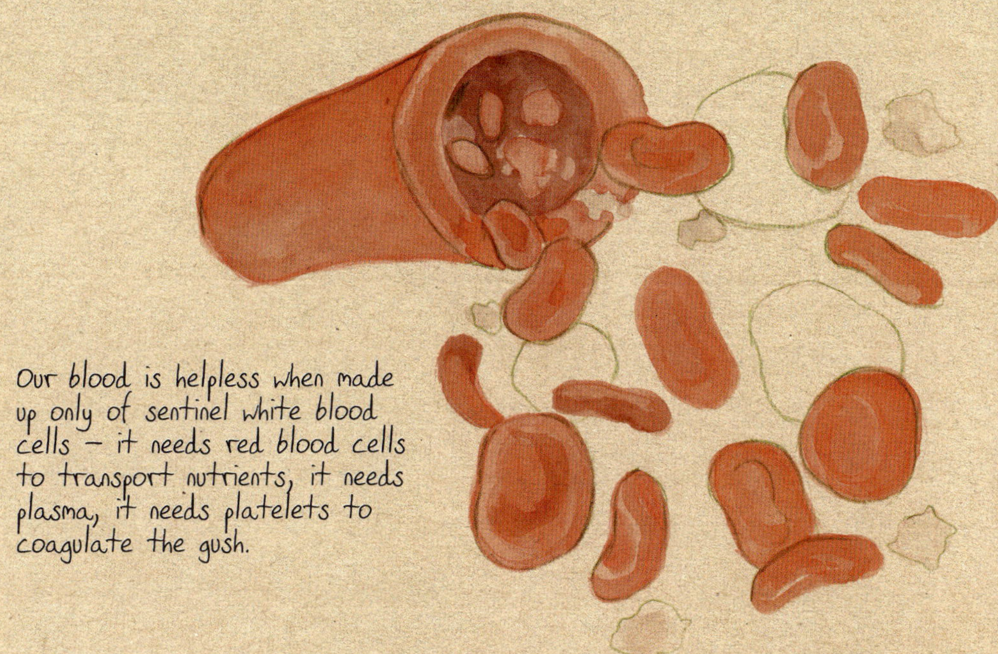

Our blood is helpless when made up only of sentinel white blood cells – it needs red blood cells to transport nutrients, it needs plasma, it needs platelets to coagulate the gush.

Even a necessary war needs paramedics and healing hands; kind eyes to ease the pain of both sides. It would be hard, even for the victorious, to survive a world without these.

They say now that it was inevitable, the armies would march towards one another on Kurukshetra and bring the story to closure, but the ending was never foreordained. Option A was never offered without Option B; and both options were offered to both sides. When Yudhishthir and Duryodhan made their way to Dwarka to seek Krshn's alliance* for the war, Duryodhan knew that for all his misdemeanours, he would not be denied.

*Duryodhan asked for Krshn's Narayani troops to join the Kaurav side. Yudhishthir asked for an unarmed Krshn to be the Pandavs' guide.

Arjun's arrows had never been more piquant. He had been gearing up his whole life for this moment: to be archer-supreme who'd bring the opponent to quick ruin. But just before the fighting began, in plain view, he had a meltdown. We could see them both – mortal man and divine charioteer – monkey banner billowing.
I can't see an enemy! Only the faces of people I know.
Gurus, uncles, cousins, buddies, fathers of girls who were in love with me.

He knelt in the red dust before Krshn.
They had a very quiet conversation.

Kurukshetra receded. Something spectacular and terrifying took its place. Before Arjun's eyes, Krshn transformed from familiar sakha to gaping maw.
His beloved now had neither form nor gender. He was galactic nursery and black hole. Neither particle nor wave could escape that two-pronged fate.

All life and non-life – past, present, in forms yet unconceived – spurted from that cavern. All life and non-life returned to the cavern: the death march infinitely more peaceful than the violence of living.
Arjun looked into the eyes of purpose and futility. He bowed, lifted his bow.

If fire is inevitable, what is the course of action that creatures caught in it should follow? Ought they to sit, hands in their laps, and submit to the flames? If life inhabits the bloodstream, this isn't even an option. In the face of fire, we do what we can, beat our wings hard. We try not to step atop our children in a bid to escape. Equanimity about the big picture, compassion for specifics.

Maybe the only way to end violence is to suspend all movement and starve. But then, even starvation causes untold cellular violence. You are warrior, said Krshn to Arjun, you chose that as much as it chose you. Now be the best warrior you can be and never mind the ending.

Isn't it weird that he needed a rote lesson at the eleventh hour after a lifetime of swotting?
Arjun had the moves, but he was no dancer. He was a technocrat.
No pyre burning today. The baby who was brought to us was so tiny, we just left her at the breast of the dark river.

Some of us aged ten years in those eighteen days of war. Most of us just died. Bheeshm started off leading the Kaurav army, but they would see three shifts in leadership. Drishtadyumna led the Pandav army until the end.
Day one, almost no one died.
Day two, some people died.
Day three, a steady trickle of death began.

Day five, yes, death.
Day seven, some more dying.
Day eight, more blood.

What sort of bullshit telling of a war story is this?
Did I promise you one? I can't pretend any of the details matter.
How's this: Kurukshetra looked like the ground under a gulmohar tree after heavy rains.
Nah. Lay off the poetry. Tell us about vyuhas instead.

Vyuha means formation. Relatively delicate, individually unremarkable components coming together to make a strong, purposeful whole. Some shoals of little fish unite to make a fish-shaped vyuha to scare off predators. Cells come together to make the vyuha of beast or bird, plant or man.

Chandrakala Vyuha

Without someone who has a big-picture view, a vyuha will wander aimlessly. The exaggerated sense of self-importance in individual cells makes human vyuhas more prone to ambling. Animal vyuhas are less ambitious, but more effective than human vyuhas. The ant colony is a vyuha functioning optimally. The vyuha leader doesn't operate remotely. He is part of the vyuha, but protected, as in a bone cage or a cranial dome. These rules apply, sans alteration, for vyuhas in war. I know of no vyuha that does not try to emulate organic forms. Man has not bettered nature's templates.

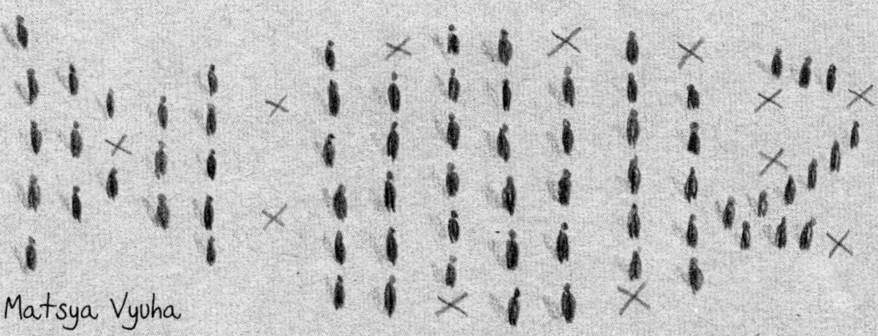

Matsya Vyuha

I was with you until this fish. This fish vyuha is a hoax. It's too dumpy-looking to be efficient.

He'll take his papa's secrets to the pyre with him, Bhainga.

Your warriors wear no armour, hold weapons limply, no elephants in the war scenes, people look different from frame to frame –

Understand the essence. The rest – whether horses were less or more and of what pedigree; whether swords were thinner or more curved – is irrelevant now.
The righteousness of mortals, upheld by law books of their own authorship, carries no weight against that basic error of judgement: disrespecting Bhoo. On Kurukshetra, Krshn overthrew the codes of men. Thunderbolt of override.

Day ten, Bheeshm laid his arms down on being faced by Shikhandi, born a woman but now a man. He was felled with a rain of arrows.
Day twelve, Arjun fought Karn for the first time.

Day thirteen, Abhimanyu pierced the Kaurav chakravyuh. He could not remember the way out. Lodged in the chakravyuh, he died –
The curse of incomplete knowledge.

Grief-mad Arjun vowed to kill the man who had shot the first arrow into his son.
Retreating to his dark place, he invoked Shiv, and received the Pashupat in his dream. He didn't have what it took to fulfil the vow - until Krshn intervened.
His sakha turned dusk to daylight. Fighting continued long on day fourteen.

Few remember that Bheem lost a son the same day. Ghatotkach, born of Hidimba, was killed by the deadliest weapon Karn had, an astra he'd been saving to kill Arjun with. Arjun lived, but guileless forest boy took the fall.
There could never be victors in this war. No good news was unclouded by grief. Vyas met the heartbroken Pandavs that night, foretold victory within five days.
On day fifteen, Yudhishthir brought news to my father of Ashwatthama's death. He didn't mention that he was speaking of an elephant by that name, not me.

My father simply laid down his arms, allowed his head to be cut off without offering any resistance. He was brought down by the lie of an honest man. A man of such high-falutin virtues that it was said his chariot floated a few inches above the ground, its horses light-footed as if they were pulling a feather. Dron was beheaded not by Arjun but by Drishtadyumn, son of Drupad.

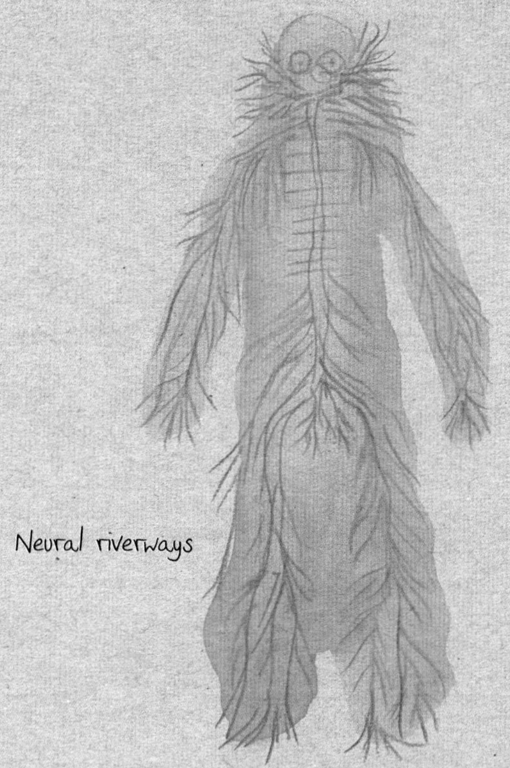


Reflex nerve action makes headless chickens scramble, makes beheaded goats kick and turn circles on the ground for as long as thirty seconds before they go still. Depending on how and where you sever the head, beheaded humans are no different. My father's head hit the ground upside down. His mouth opened and closed, twice; ocular gaze moved from me to his body, back to me, confused; then he died. That eye contact is still my undoing. I vowed to avenge Dron's death.

A thorough, hypnotic fire – just like the countless ones I have warmed my hands at – licked my father's chassis clean. May we never squander the chance of looking at mortality – others' and our own – unflinchingly.

On day seventeen, Bheem killed Dusshasan and drank straight from his carotid.
Karn-Arjun collided. Parshuram's curse came true. Arjun killed Karn.

The last day of the battle, the eighteenth, the bloodiest.
With the exception of Duryodhan, me, my uncle Kripa and Kritvarma – every last Kaurav and Kaurav ally returned their blood to Kurukshetra.

Some worlds ago, Indra took submarine refuge. He travelled down the stem of a lotus, remained hidden for aeons, until he had repented for his ways. He was allowed to stay there until he was ready to surface.

Injured and weak, Duryodhan took refuge at the bottom of a lake too. Bheem hunted him down, challenged a dying man to combat, battered his thighs to pulp.

# SAUPTIK

Later that night, it was Shiv I invoked.
If Arjun had served as Mahavishnu's arm, I, Aswatthama, was Shiv's arm. The arm of Mahadev did indeed slip in where there had only been a bloodied stump before. It was Shiv's dagger I wielded, it was his ganas who watched over me, their terrible faces flickering in my own.

My victims didn't even wake up when my blade touched skin. Light blade, strong male bodies spasming helplessly. It set off synaptic fireworks in my head.
Each stab was an orgasm. Orgasm after orgasm after orgasm.

Admire that blood ritual for what it was: a job well executed. They were so many, I was one. On the stage of that new moon night, I dazzled like never before. For the only time in my life, I was truly magnificent.

They were harrowed but fed, one night away from returning to their living wives. I was harrowed and hungry, with no one and nothing to return to. On the sons and kin of Draupadi, flopped in their camp beds, I lavished the proud precision of a jeweller. I laid waste to their entire camp with grace. No mess, only a slim smile welling up with blood on each throat. Heads fell off bodies, effortless as flowers.

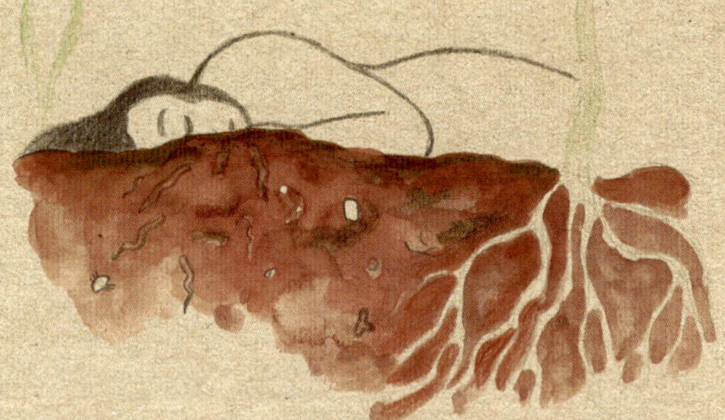

There weren't enough living people with their wits about them, to cremate the dead of Kurukshetra. Even the soil acknowledged surfeit, sticky with clotted blood. Raptors diligently circled the sky, worms turned the earth – but the glut was too much, their numbers too few. Bodies bloated, the air grew putrid; finally it was left to the microbes to take charge of the situation and break the carcasses down to their constituents.

You killed the poor sons of Draupadi instead of wiping out the Pandavs!
You messed up!
Avenging my father meant wiping out Drupad's lineage: the man himself, his sons, his grandsons.
The Pandavs didn't figure on the hit list. Their sons' throats slit, there wasn't any need to put a blade to an ageing Draupadi.

While I sent their sons across the Vaitarni, the Pandavs – and Krshn – slept under the stars, on the banks of Oghavati, the oozing one, arm of Yamuna.
She was dark as Kaliyug, metallic as blood, swollen with viscera and half-burnt bodies – there weren't enough trees left for funeral pyres.
So dense were Oghavati's waters, she flowed sluggish as oil.

Hastinapur had fallen silent. No one had the will to take on the grief of another. Widows ran out of tears. Draupadi's hair looked and smelled like the Oghavati too. A young handmaiden struggled with a comb full of clots.

This strand is combed through with the blood of Dusshasan.

This strand, with the blood of Duryodhan.

This strand – Dron, Karn, Bheeshm, Shakuni, Jayadrath, and every last Kaurav there was.

This strand is combed through with the blood of your father, your twin, your five sons.

No coiffure more expensive in the known history of mortals.

GREATEST ACT OF COMPASSION

The curse of incomplete knowledge.
Revoke your astras before they destroy your world!
Arjun revoked his Pashupat. I wasn't able to revoke mine. Krshn reached out, plucked the jewel out of my forehead. Then he held out his palm to show me.
No ruby of clear, sparkling notes. It was a spent piece of coal.

There's something I must ask you.
Arjun walked next to your greatness for so long but never understood it –
Duryodhan was braver than he, Karn kinder, Bheem more humble. Why did Father love Arjun most? Why did you?

Did my father foil my ambition – and Eklavya's and Karn's – so that he could save us all from Arjun's ultimately-tragic fate?
Was Arjun your chosen sakha because he followed instructions best? Because he needed one-on-one attention the most?

Tell me this, O Krshn, and take the last of my burning away –
What is so great about a man who can only see the left eye of a wooden bird when a glorious forest lies beyond?

Nothing at all.
As a cow gazes at her calf, that is how Krshn gazed at me.

To recognize acts of love where they went unrecognized before...
Narayan wants of Nara only that he be Nara: human, not superhuman.
Arjun knew when to ask for help.

How brightly this tree burns! When the carnage is over, you may ache for what was set afire in haste. Check for the seeds buried under the ash. As for me, I think I have earned my long sleep.

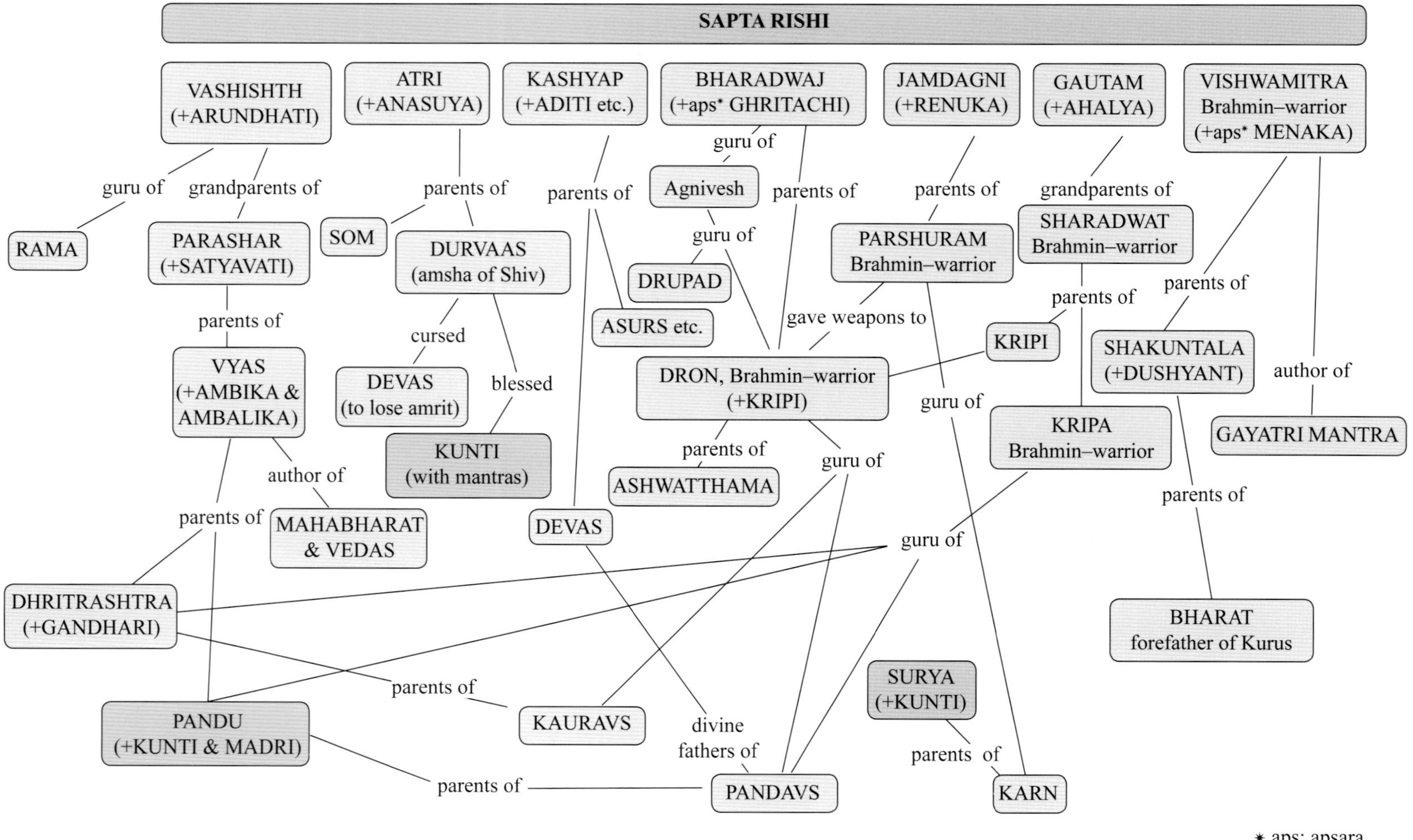
SAPTA RISHI
VASHISHTH (+ARUNDHATI)
ATRI (+ANASUYA)
KASHYAP (+ADITI etc.)
BHARADWAJ (+aps* GHRITACHI)
JAMDAGNI (+RENUKA)
GAUTAM (+AHALYA)
VISHWAMITRA Brahmin–warrior (+aps* MENAKA)
guru of
grandparents of
parents of
parents of
guru of
Agnivesh
parents of
parents of
grandparents of
RAMA
PARASHAR (+SATYAVATI)
SOM
DURVAAS (amsha of Shiv)
guru of
DRUPAD
PARSHURAM Brahmin–warrior
SHARADWAT Brahmin–warrior
parents of
parents of
parents of
ASURS etc.
gave weapons to
KRIPI
cursed
SHAKUNTALA (+DUSHYANT)
author of
VYAS (+AMBIKA & AMBALIKA)
DEVAS (to lose amrit)
blessed
DRON, Brahmin–warrior (+KRIPI)
guru of
KRIPA Brahmin–warrior
GAYATRI MANTRA
KUNTI (with mantras)
parents of
author of
ASHWATTHAMA
guru of
parents of
parents of
MAHABHARAT & VEDAS
DEVAS
guru of
DHRITRASHTRA (+GANDHARI)
BHARAT forefather of Kurus
SURYA (+KUNTI)
parents of
KAURAVS
divine fathers of
PANDU (+KUNTI & MADRI)
parents of
parents of
PANDAVS
KARN
* aps: apsara

# AUTHOR'S NOTE

Hopeless kings have been served by exemplary men. Children of sages reveal themselves to be fools; children of cowards prove to be warriors. There's simply no saying who will birth what.

The buck stops with you.

It is as easy and as excruciatingly hard as that.

Amruta Patil
August 2016

# GLOSSARY

**Sauptik:** 'Those who are sleeping'; tenth of the Mahabharat's eighteen books.

**Abhimanyu:** Son of Arjun and Subhadra; husband of Uttara.

**Acharya:** Preceptor.

**Agni:** Fire god.

**Amrit:** Elixir of immortality; blissfire; appeared during the churning of the ocean when devas and asurs churned in tandem. Devas were allowed to drink amrit, asurs were not.

**Apsara:** Water nymph (apa = water). Apsaras often serve as allies of the devas in maintaining the balance in the three worlds.

**Arghya:** Libations offered to gods, rishis, elders.

**Arjun:** Third Pandav; the archer; also known as Dhananjay and Sabyasaachi; biological son of Indra and Pritha; husband of Draupadi, Chitrangada, Subhadra.

**Ashram:** Abode of the guru; also stations of life (Brahmachaarya, Grihasta, Sanyaas).

**Ashwatthama:** 'One who neighs like a horse'; son of acharya Dron and Kripi.

**Asur:** Older brothers and arch rivals of the devas; dissonant forces.

**Atharva Ved:** First Indic text dealing with medicine; identifies the causes of disease as living causative agents (yatudhāna, kimīdin, kṛmi, durṇāma) to be countered by incantation and plant-based drugs.

**Avatar:** Reincarnations of Vishnu; various avatars include Matsya (fish), Kurma (turtle), Varaha (boar), Narsimha (man–lion), Vaman (dwarf), Parshuram (axe-wielding brahmin), Ram (just ruler, ideal king) and Krshn (strategist, statesman).

**Bali:** Asur who challenged Indra Purandara and became the next Indra.

**Bansuri:** Seven- or eight-holed traverse flute made of bamboo; associated with Krshn; a smaller version of the bansuri is known as the Venu or Murali.

**Bharadwaj:** Lineage of Dron and Ashwatthama; also a name for the crow pheasant in some Indian languages.

**Bheem:** Second Pandav; powerful wrestler; mace-exponent; brother of Hanuman (common biological father: Vayu).

**Bheeshm:** Elder of the Kuru clan; son of Shantanu and Ganga; sworn to celibacy.

**Bholenath:** 'Naïve/Innocent One'; another name for Shiv.

**Bhoo Devi:** Earth goddess.

**Bhoomi:** Land; ground beneath the feet.

**Brahmin:** Person who has dedicated his life to learning, reining in the senses, dissipating knowledge without hope of profit.

**Braj bhoomi:** Settlement of herders and cattle breeders.

**Chakra:** Spiral; wheel.

**Chiranjeevi:** 'One with long life'; the seven chiranjeevis are the asur Bali, Vyas, Hanuman, Ravan's brother Vibhishan, the axe-wielding Parshuram, Kripa and Ashwatthama.

**Chitrangada:** Princess and ruler of Manipur; wife of Arjun; mother of his son Babruvahan.

**Daan:** Charity.

**Dadhichi:** Rishi whose spine was used to make Indra's weapon, Vajra, that killed Vritra.

**Daksha:** Foremost prajapati; father of Sati (among many others); grandfather of most living beings.

**Dama:** Restraint.

**Damru:** Small two-headed drum associated with Shiv.

**Dayaa:** Compassion.

**Dev:** Younger brothers of the asurs; consonant forces.

**Devaki:** Mother of Krshn; wife of Vasudev; sister of Kamsa.

**Devlok:** Abode of the devas.

**Dhritrashtra:** Blind brother of Pandu; king of Hastinapur; husband of Gandhari, father of the Kauravs.

**Dron:** Preceptor of the Kuru princes; father of Ashwatthama; husband of Kripi.

**Draupadi:** Fireborn daughter of King Drupad; Drishtadyumn's twin; Shikhandi's sister; wife of the five Pandavs; mother of Prativindhya (with Yudhishthir), Sutasom (with Bheem), Shrutakarm (with Arjun), Shatanik (with Nakul) and Shrutasen (with Sahdev).

**Drishtadyumn:** Fireborn son of King Drupad; Draupadi's twin; Shikhandi's brother.

**Drupad:** King of Panchal; husband of Prishati; father of Shikhandi, Draupadi and Drishtadyumn.

**Dom:** Community engaged in the cremation of dead bodies in India; the dom provides the first set of five logs of wood required for the funeral pyre and hands over the lighted straw to the person who will start the funeral pyre.

**Duryodhan:** Prince of Hastinapur; oldest son of Dhritrashtra and Gandhari.

**Dusshasan:** One of the Kauravs; Duryodhan's closest sibling.

**Eklavya:** Boy from the forest-dwelling nishad tribe; ace archer.

**Gana:** Attendants and foot soldiers of Shiv, consisting of outliers such as bhootas, nagas, pishaachas, rakshasas, guhyakas, gandharvas and siddhas, among others.

**Gandhari:** Queen of Hastinapur; wife of Dhritrashtra; mother of the Kauravs; sister of Shakuni.

**Gandiv:** Arjun's bow.

**Ganga:** Part of the great triad of river goddesses (with Saraswati and Yamuna); mother of Bheeshm.

**Ghee:** Clarified butter made from cow's milk; of great medicinal worth; known as toop/tuppa in some Indian languages.

**Gokul:** 'Abode of cows'; home of the gopas and gopis.

**Gopal:** Protector of cows; name for Krshn.

**Gopi** (f)/**Gopa** (m): Person who looks after cows.

**Govardhan:** Sacred mountain of Gokul.

**Guna:** Three inherent human qualities, present in different permutation-combinations in most people. Sattva (wisdom/imparts balance), Rajas (energy/can bring imbalance and a tendency towards excess), Tamas (substance/can bring inertia).

**Gurudakshina:** A teacher's fee, monetary or otherwise, to be paid at the end of one's Education.

**Gurukul:** 'Abode of the guru' where disciples (shishya) lived, served, learned.

**Hanuman:** Monkey-god; older brother of Bheem; son of Vayu and Anjana.

**Hastinapur:** Capital of the Kuru dynasty.

**Hidimba:** Rakshasi; wife of Bheem; mother of Bheem's son Ghatotkach.

**Houses of life:** Three ashrams or stages of human life: Brahmachaarya, Grihasta and Sanyaas.

**Indra:** Title for the foremost among devas; Indra Purandara was Arjun's biological father.

**Indraprasth:** 'Abode of Indra'; the Pandav capital, with Yudhishthir as king.

**Iti Iti:** 'This! And This!'.

**Kailash:** High mountain retreat of Shiv and Sati.

**Kalpa:** Aeon; period of time between the creation and recreation of worlds.

**Kamadhenu:** 'Wish-granting cow' born during the churning of the ocean; belongs to Vashishth rishi.

**Kamsa:** King of Mathura; brother of Devaki; kept Devaki and her husband in captivity.

**Karmabhoomi:** 'Field where one's karma must play out'.

**Karn:** Oldest son of Pritha (through Surya); half-brother of the Pandavs; foster son of charioteer Adhirath and his wife, Radha.

**Khandav-van:** Primeval forest that was cleared by Arjun and Krshn to make way for Indraprasth.

**Kripi:** Wife of Dron; twin sister of Kripa; mother of Ashwatthama.

**Krshn:** Avatar of Vishnu during the Dwapar Yug; son of Vasudev and Devaki, adopted by Nand and Yashoda; maternal cousin of the Pandavs.

**Kunti:** Mother of the Pandavs Yudhishthir, Bheem and Arjun; see 'Pritha'.

**Kuru:** Ancestor of the Kauravs and Pandavs.

**Kurukshetra:** Field where the eighteen-day battle between the Kaurav and Pandav allies took place.

**Leela:** Divine play.

**Madri:** Pandu's second wife; mother of twins Nakul and Sahdev.

**Mahadev:** Shiv.

**Mantra:** Incantation.

**Maya:** Illusion; architect of Indraprasth; meister of illusion and craftsmanship.

**Meru:** Primordial mountain that served as the axis for the churning.

**Mithai**: Indian sweets.

**Mrityulok:** Realm of mortals (mrityu = death, lok = abode).

**Naglok:** Underwater abode of the magical serpents, the nagas.

**Nakshatra:** Constellation.

**Nakul:** Youngest Pandav; Sahdev's twin; son of Madri and the Ashwin twins.

**Nand:** Cowherd; husband of Yashoda; foster father of Krshn.

**Nar:** Sage who was Narayan's mortal companion; Arjun was said to be Nar to Krshn's Narayan.

**Narad:** Devotee of Narayan/Vishnu; celibate sage who travels between the worlds ferrying warning and praise of Vishnu.

**Narayan:** Vishnu; etymologically connected to his reclining on water.

**Narayani:** Armed warrior army belonging to Vishnu (Narayan).

**Neti Neti:** 'Not This, Not This'.

**Nishad:** Forest-dwelling tribe that is the natural enemy of inhabitation and empire.

**Oghavati:** 'Oozing one'; tributary of the Yamuna river, next to which the Pandavs camped when the Kurukshetra battle was over.

**Pandu:** Son of Ambalika and Vyas; husband of Kunti and Madri; foster father of the Pandavs.

**Parvati:** Consort of Shiv; daughter of Himavat and apsara Menaka; reincarnation of Sati.

**Parshuram**: Avatar of Vishnu; axe-wielding brahmin who swore to destroy all rajanyas; guru of Karn.

**Pashupat:** Shiv's weapon.

**Pashupati:** Another name for Shiv (pashu = yoked beasts, pati = leader).

**Pootana:** Vishakanya (poison maiden) sent by King Kamsa to kill baby Krshn.

**Prajapati:** Lords of the people; of whom Daksha was one.

**Prishati:** King Drupad's wife; Shikhandi's mother.

**Pritha:** 'Wide as the earth'; another name for Kunti; mother of the Pandavs Yudhishthir (through Dharm), Bheem (through Vayu) and Arjun (through Indra); and of Karn (through Surya).

**Prithu:** King after whom Prithvi, the earth, is named.

**Prithvi:** Earth.

**Purushottam:** Excellent man.

**Radha:** Gopi from Braj; Krshn's first love, she was much older than him.

**Rajanya:** Person who has dedicated his life to guarding and legislating the land.

**Rakshasa:** Powerful, fierce warriors and illusionists; often cannibalistic and forest-dwelling.

**Ranabhoomi:** 'Battlefield'.

**Rangabhoomi:** 'Playing field'.

**Rathi:** Warrior who fights from atop a chariot (ratha).

**Rishi:** Seer; according to Tārānātha, who compiled the great Sanskrit dictionary, 'ṛṣati jñānena saṃsāra-pāram' (i.e., 'one who reaches beyond this mundane world by means of spiritual knowledge').

**Sahdev:** Youngest Pandav; Nakul's twin brother; son of Madri and the Ashwin twins.

**Sakha** (m)/**Sakhi** (f): 'The true one'; close companion.

**Sanjeevni:** Also 'Mritasanjeevni'; esoteric knowledge that could help revive the dead; belonged to the asurs, thanks to their preceptor Shukra.

**Saranga bird:** Possibly cuckoo.

**Saraswati:** One of the great triad of river goddesses (with Ganga and Yamuna), who disappeared underground.

**Sati:** Daughter of Daksha; first wife of Shiv; also known as Dakshayini.

**Sattva:** See 'Guna'.

**Satyavati:** Matriarch and queen of Hastinapur; wife of Shantanu; mother of Vyas rishi; grandmother of Pandu and Dhritrashtra.

**Shaastra:** Treatise; scriptures; the education of princes consisted, among other things, of studying Dharma Shaastra (right, wrong, greyscale of dharma), Artha Shaastra (economics), Shilp Shaastra (art, craft) and Dhanurveda (martial skills).

**Shakuni:** 'Ominous'; expert gambler; brother of Queen Gandhari.

**Shastra:** Armament.

**Shikhandi:** Transgender (ftm) son of King Drupad and Prishati; oldest daughter of King Drupad; half-sibling of Draupadi; said to be a reincarnation of Amba, princess of Kashi.

**Shishupal:** Prince of Chedi; cousin of Krshn (through his paternal aunt).

**Shiv:** 'Pure'; also known as Mahadev, Pashupati, Bholenath; consort of Sati, Parvati.

**Shree Devi:** Goddess of wealth and bounty; also known as Lakshmi.

**Siddhi:** Spiritual powers said to be obtained by tapasya, control of the senses, devotion, pranayama or good birth.

**Smashan:** Charnel ground.

**Snatak:** Brahmin students who have just completed their education, recent graduates.

**Subhadra:** 'One with good brothers'; sister of Krshn and Balram; wife of Arjun; mother of Abhimanyu.

**Sudarshan Chakra:** One of Vishnu's armaments/attributes; the wheel of time.

**Sukshmata:** Finesse; nuance.

**Sutradhaar:** 'Thread-bearer'; storyteller.

**Swaha:** 'So be it'; 'well said'; denouement indicating the end of a mantra.

**Tapasya**: Penance, ardour.

**Tirth:** 'Crossing place, ford'; destination for pilgrims.

**Upside-down tree:** Metaphor that symbolizes the world of mortals (sustained by roots in the heavens, the upside-down tree fruits on the earth); as also the human body (the brain-roots nourishing the limb-branches below).

**Van:** Forest.

**Vaikunth:** Abode of Vishnu.

**Vajra:** Indra's weapon made of Dadhichi's spine; thunderbolt.

**Varna:** Denomination based on profession.

**Vashishth:** Rishi; one of the navigators of the multiverse; Vishwamitra's main rival.

**Vasudev:** Father of Krshn; brother of Pritha; husband of Devaki.

**Vasudev Paundraka:** Man who plagiarized Krshn's insignia and claimed his status.

**Vidur:** Half-brother of Dhritrashtra and Pandu (common father: Vyas); advisor to King Dhritrashtra.

**Vinata:** Mother of solar raptors Arun and Garud; sister of Kadru (mother of serpents), both were wives of Kashyap rishi.

**Vishkanya:** Mythic female assassins; administered steadily increasing doses of poison from infancy onwards, they are resistant to poison but their bodies are so toxic, they can bring about someone's death by a kiss or by suckling them.

**Vishwamitra:** King-turned-rishi; one of the navigators of the multiverse; Vashishth's main rival; father of Shakuntala (through apsara Menaka).

**Vishwaroop:** 'Cosmic form'; revealed by the avatar Krshn a couple of times during the Mahabharat.

**Vritra:** Magical winged serpent; also known as Ahi; created by Tvastra; foe of Indra.

**Vyas:** Rishi; compiler of the Mahabharat; son of Parasher and Satyavati; forefather of the Kaurav princes.

**Vyuha:** Formation (military, etc).

**Yadav:** Tribe that Krshn was born into.

**Yagna:** Sacrifice made to Agni.

**Yamuna:** One of the great triad of river goddesses (with Ganga and Saraswati); also known as Yami; twin sister of Yama, god of right conduct and of death.

**Yantra:** Instrument.

**Yashoda:** Wife of Nand; foster mother of Krshn.

**Yog:** Union; yoking together of body, mind and senses.

**Yudhishthir:** Eldest Pandav; king of Indraprasth; biological son of Dharm and Pritha.

**Yug:** Each of the four stages of the cycles of time: Krita, Treta, Dwapar and Kali; the names of the four yugas correspond with those of dice thrown.

# SUGGESTED READING


Bibek Debroy (trans.), *The Mahabharata* (Volumes 1–8), New Delhi: Penguin Books India, 2010–2015

Bibek Debroy and Dipavali Debroy, *The Holy Puranas* (Volumes 1–3), New Delhi: BR Publishing Corporation, 2002

B.K.S. Iyengar, *Tree of Yoga*, London: Harper Thorsons, 2013

Cain Carroll and Revital Carroll, *Mudras of India: A Comprehensive Guide to the Hand Gestures of Yoga and Indian Dance*, London: Singing Dragon, 2012

Diana L. Eck, *India: A Sacred Geography*, New York: Harmony Books, 2012

Edward P. Rice, *The Mahabharata: Analysis and Index*, London: Humphrey Milford, 1934

Eugen Herrigel, *Zen in the Art of Archery*, New York: Vintage Books, 1999

Frits Staal, *Discovering the Vedas*, New Delhi: Penguin Books India, 2008

H. David Coulter, *Anatomy of Hatha Yoga*, Pennsylvania: Body and Breath, 2001

Joseph S. Alter, *The Wrestler's Body*, Berkeley: University of California Press, 1992

Kamala Subramaniam, *Shrimad Bhagavatam*, New Delhi: Bharatiya Vidya Bhavan, 2006

Roberto Calasso, *Ardor*, New York: Farrar, Straus and Giroux, 2014

Surinder Mohan Bharadwaj, *Hindu Places of Pilgrimage in India*, Berkeley: University of California Press, 1973

T.K.V. Desikachar, *The Heart of Yoga: Developing a Personal Practice*, Vermont: Inner Traditions International, 1995

Wendy Doniger, *On Hinduism*, New Delhi: Aleph Book Company, 2013

Ananda K. Coomaraswamy, 'The Symbolism of Archery', *Studies in Comparative Religion*, Vol. 5, No. 2, Spring 1971

Inderjit Badhwar, 'Varanasi: The dues of death', *India Today*, 15 April 1986

R. Alexander Medin, '3 Gurus, 48 Questions', *Namarupa*, Fall 2004

# GRATITUDE

Prashant Trivedi, for many things, but most importantly for teaching me the difference between 'elder' and 'older', and what it really means to live in synchronicity with the elements. Chogyam Trungpa Rinpoche, for the playful switchblade that is Crazy Wisdom. Juan-Manuel Fuentes, for opening the portal of yog to me. Bibek Debroy for his translations of the Mahabharat and the Puranas, and for generous troubleshooting. Devdutt Pattanaik, for asking the playful, transforming question, 'Ranabhoomi, ya rangabhoomi?' and for leading me to the story about Draupadi's coiffure.

These influences, among innumerable others, mark the DNA of *Sauptik*: The luminous palette of Nicholas Roerich and Pierre Bonnard. The masterful compositions of Diego Rivera. The forests of Henri Rousseau. The scientific passion-prose of William Bryant Logan's book *Dirt: Ecstatic Skin of the Earth*.

For conversational push/pull that enriched facets of this work, thank you, Jayaprakash Satyamurthy, Mandakini Pachauri, Anita Kamath Dudhane, Chintan Girish Modi, Hinano Reia, Anuja Chauhan, Ajit Kulkarni, Punam Zutshi. Mohinish Shukla, for fixing bad science and logical fallacies. Joël Riou, for input on classical dance, Mahabharat genealogy. My Sanskrit helpline – Ramanuja Devanathan, Eric M. Gurevitch, Arjun Chaudhuri, Rohini Bakshi. Sumana Roy, for botanical counsel. Anaël Seghezzi, Matt Madden, Janine Shroff, Sridhar Rajan, Sanjeev Kumar (HarperCollins), Basant Kumar Choudhary (Thomson Press) for technical support. Sohini Basak and Shreya Ila Anasuya, for proofreading assistance. Duraisamy Balaguru, for gen on neurological reflex in cadavers; Karan Manral, Yogita Mehra, Poonam Bir Kasturi, on gardening and compost. Iggy Ahluwalia, for giving me a digital bookshelf when I needed it most. Danielle Seghezzi, for supplying me with found images for collage. Rohit Chawla, for taking the author photo in a setting close to my heart.

There's something profoundly important about investing in living artists instead of dead ones. Vijay Chowgule, Vini Tandon Keni, Vivek Menezes, Aparna Jain, Sonia Jabbar: your buying my artwork originals afforded me a peaceful year of working on *Sauptik*. The project was partially enabled by financial grants from Centre National du Livre (CNL) and Villa Marguerite Yourcenar, Nord Pas Calais, France. La Maison des Auteurs, Angouleme, served as studio-womb where most work on the two Parva books was completed. Special thanks to Pilar Munoz and Brigitte Macias for ironing out innumerable logistical creases during my time there.

Thank you, V.K. Karthika and HarperCollins India: safe, beloved literary home.

For expressive love and steadfast friendship: Brinda Datta, Cynthia Green, Raashmi Chakravarti, S.K. and Kabir Saxena, Amrita Narayanan, Yasmine Claire, Deboleena Rakshit, Shreya Ila Anasuya, Yashodhan Ghorpade, K.T. Sandip. Arun, Alka and Ajey Patil, for samsaric anchoring. Tender gratitude to Anaël Seghezzi, hermit love, whose sagesse doesn't hanker for surround-sound or big stage.

First published in hardback in India in 2016 by
HarperCollins *Publishers* India
A-75, Sector 57, Noida, Uttar Pradesh 201301, India
harpercollins.co.in

This edition published in India by HarperCollins *Publishers* in 2021



P-ISBN: 978-93-5422-936-7
E-ISBN: 978-93-5264-065-2



Typeset in FG Amura
Design and Layout by Amruta Patil

This project was supported by the Cité Internationale de la Bande Dessinée et de l'Image and its artist residency programme at La Maison des Auteurs (Angoulême, France).

Printed and bound at
Thomson Press (India) Ltd